7/16   FICTION

P9-CEJ-644

$28.95

THE FAIRBAIRN FORTUNES

Recent Titles from Una-Mary Parker from Severn House

ALEXIA'S SECRETS
ECHOES OF BETRAYAL

The Granville Series
THE GRANVILLE SISTERS
THE GRANVILLE AFFAIRE
THE GRANVILLE LEGACY

The Fairbairn Series
THE FAIRBAIRN GIRLS
THE FAIRBAIRN FORTUNES

THE FAIRBAIRN FORTUNES

Una-Mary Parker

severn
House

This first world edition published 2016
in Great Britain and the USA by
SEVERN HOUSE PUBLISHERS LTD of
19 Cedar Road, Sutton, Surrey, England, SM2 5DA.
Trade paperback edition first published
in Great Britain and the USA 2016 by
SEVERN HOUSE PUBLISHERS LTD

British Library Cataloguing in Publication Data

Parker, Una-Mary author.
  The Fairbairn fortunes.
  1. Aristocracy (Social class)–Fiction. 2. Great Britain–
  Social life and customs–20th century–Fiction. 3. Great
  Britain–History–George V, 1910-1936–Fiction.
  4. Domestic fiction.
  I. Title
  823.9'14-dc23

ISBN-13: 978-0-7278-8590-6 (cased)
ISBN-13: 978-1-84751-693-0 (trade paper)
ISBN-13: 978-1-78010-753-0 (e-book)

All Severn House titles are printed on acid-free paper.

Severn House Publishers support the Forest Stewardship Council™ [FSC™],
the leading international forest certification organisation.
All our titles that are printed on FSC certified paper carry the FSC logo.

Typeset by Palimpsest Book Production Ltd.,
Falkirk, Stirlingshire, Scotland.
Printed and bound in Great Britain by
TJ International, Padstow, Cornwall.

One

Cranley Court, 1913

'Darling Laura! I'm so glad you arrived before the others,' Diana exclaimed, hurrying forward to kiss her sister. 'Come and sit by the fire in the library. I want to hear all your news. And how are you, Caroline?'

She bent down to hug her nine-year-old niece. 'Archie and Emily are so excited at having you to stay.'

Caroline, pretty and bright-eyed, gazed up at her favourite aunt in silent awe, not knowing what to say.

Laura smiled encouragingly and murmured, 'Say hello to Aunt Di, darling.' Then she straightened her back, looking tired. 'I thought we'd never get here. There was snow on the line and we were held up for ages.' As she spoke she put down her fur muff and started taking off her small, chic hat.

'You're here now and that's the main thing,' Diana said soothingly. 'Caroline, why don't you run up to the playroom and surprise the others? With all this snow on the drive, I don't think they heard you arrive.'

The child was staring wide-eyed at the splendid Christmas tree with its quaint Victorian decorations that had been in the Kelso family for two generations. The small, carved and painted animals, miniature bugles and stars had been hung artfully from the dense pine branches and there were even cream-coloured candles held in place by little metal clips.

'It's beautiful, Di,' Laura exclaimed. 'It must have taken you hours to decorate.'

Diana laughed. 'Mrs Armstrong and I did it after the children had gone to bed. We didn't finish until about two in the morning! Their faces were priceless the next day. Emily wondered if Father Christmas had delivered it.'

'Thank God for Mrs Armstrong,' Laura observed, *sotto voce.*

'I wish we'd had such a good housekeeper when we were young. Poor Mama wasn't exactly artistic, was she?'

Diana nodded. 'That's what happens if you have eleven children. I look back on those days of living in a big castle and wonder how Mama managed to keep the staff we had. Do you remember how cold it was? Even in summer? Living in a house, even a big one like this, is so easy by comparison. Now, let's get you settled in.'

She turned to Burton and at a signal the butler gave the first footman orders to take Lady Laura Leighton-Harvey's luggage up to her room, where one of the chambermaids would do her unpacking. Meanwhile, Mrs Armstrong had already taken Caroline up to the playroom where Nanny Kelso was about to preside over nursery tea, while the cousins eyed each other with silent curiosity and suspicion. Caroline couldn't help feeling inferior when she stayed at Cranley Court. In fact, she felt inferior when she stayed with any of her mother's sisters. They were all rich. They all had big houses and servants – even Aunt Georgie, who'd scandalized Scottish society by marrying an Irish working-class man who owned several pubs. Every one of her many cousins also had a father they could see every day; respectable men who didn't get drunk and hadn't been thrown into an institution. No one really mentioned her father these days, and that hurt her a lot. It was as if he'd brought shame on the family. No one asked after him or mentioned his name, and yet they talked about the other uncles. He might have been dead for all they cared.

Caroline knew he'd spent all their money and it was called 'going bankrupt', but Mama earned money with her dress-making so why couldn't Dada live with them? Why did he live with his sister?

'Come along, Caroline,' said Nanny Kelso. 'You'll fade away if you don't eat something.'

Caroline put on what she considered to be her rather grand and grown-up voice. 'I'm not hungry, thank you very much.'

'You won't thank me if you get ill,' Nanny retorted sturdily. 'Now, come along. Eat your bread and butter and then you can have a nice slice of Dundee cake.'

While Caroline nibbled with reluctance, Archie, who was two years older, decided to engage her in stilted conversation.

'How is Edinburgh?'

'It's still standing,' she replied, glancing balefully at him.

'Is Aunt Laura still making dresses?' Emily enquired curiously.

She's a designer, not a common dressmaker,' Caroline said rudely.

Nanny sighed inwardly and raised her eyes to heaven. It was going to be a very long Christmas holiday at this rate. Caroline was offended by everything that was said to her. Her Ladyship had warned her it was better not to mention Mr Leighton-Harvey in front of his daughter, because this would be the third festive season when he'd remained with his sister. He'd made no contact with Caroline; not even a Christmas card.

It was Nanny's private belief that Caroline was the most spoilt little girl she'd ever known. Lady Laura pandered to her one moment and then scolded her the next because she could turn nasty in a flash. For all her prettiness she was a treacherous child who needed a firm hand, in Nanny's opinion.

Downstairs, Diana and Laura were sitting by the crackling log fire in the book-lined library, which had two French windows leading on to a terrace, and beyond, the snow-covered lawns of Diana's large estate in Perthshire.

To Laura, Cranley Court had become a sanctuary. It was the only place that occurred to her to flee to with Caroline when Walter had become bankrupt. The only place where she could afford to take the train to. The only place where kindness and understanding were generously given by both Diana and her husband, Robert. The sheer comfort and warmth of the house and the scent of smouldering pine logs made her feel as if she was drifting into paradise, where she could forget about working for up to eighteen hours a day in a cold, rented flat in Edinburgh.

'Let's have some tea,' Diana was saying. 'The others won't be here for ages. I want to hear all your news. How is the business going?'

Her sister looked older: there were fine lines on her face

and her dark hair had lost its lustre. But her hazel eyes were as spirited as ever, and when she smiled her whole face lit up.

'I'm doing quite well,' she replied. 'I'll be able to repay your loan by Easter . . .'

Diana raised her slender hand in protest. 'You don't have to, my dear. I want to make sure you're really all right financially. There's absolutely no hurry.'

'Thank you, but I'd like to,' Laura protested. 'Once again, Mrs Sutherland, who got me going the first time, has contacted all my old clients as well as new ones to get their wardrobes made by me. She really knows what to say to the "ladies of Edinburgh" to persuade them to buy their clothes from me!'

'So your former assistant, Helen, who bought the business from you when you got married – she didn't want to join forces once more?'

Laura's mouth tightened. 'Unfortunately not. I offered to buy her out but she was quite nasty. In a way I can understand. She now looks upon me as a rival who will steal all my old clients from her. But I did start the business in the first place and I did let her have it for a song.' She sighed.

'Does this make it awkward for Mrs Sutherland?'

'No, because when I left she stopped finding clients for Helen. Just imagine! Helen refused to give her a commission!' Laura started laughing. 'Dear old Mrs Sutherland is thrilled I'm back. I also pay her to fetch Caroline from school every afternoon, which is a great help.'

Diana leaned back in her chair and looked at her elder sister with admiration. 'Good for you. I'm so glad it's all going so well.' Then she smiled indulgently. 'And how is Caroline getting on at ballet school? Is she still determined to be a dancer?' She covered her eyes with her hand in mock horror and giggled. 'Have you told Mama that her granddaughter wants to be a dancer? My dear, she'll have a heart attack on the spot.'

'I'll cross that bridge when I come to it,' Laura retorted, crossing her fingers. 'Caroline is determined and she's very talented. Her ballet teacher thinks she should start training seriously at some point with Madame Judith Espinosa.'

Diana raised her eyebrows. 'That is serious.'

'I know. She thinks Caroline has great potential.'

'Did you know that Lizzie and Humphrey have bought a house in London? Apparently it's near the Victoria and Albert Museum.'

Laura nodded. 'I'm dying to see her and hear all about it. So who is staying here for Christmas? I haven't seen any of the family for so long.'

'All of them,' Diana replied in a low voice.

'All of them?' Laura looked stunned. 'Where will they all sleep? I know you've got over thirty bedrooms, but isn't it going to be rather a crush?'

Diana looked unperturbed. 'I'm putting all the very little ones in the night nursery. Some will have to sleep on camp beds but they'll be fine.'

Laura's eyes widened. 'There will be complete chaos when they all wake up on Christmas morning and find that Father Christmas paid them a visit in the night. Have you thought this through, Di?' She started laughing. 'How is Father Christmas going to know which child is which if they're asleep higgledy-piggledy all over the place? Supposing . . . you know . . . he trips over the camp beds . . .?' Overcome with mirth and unable to continue, Laura leaned back in her chair, helpless with laughter at the thought of Father Christmas stumbling around in the pitch dark.

Diana started giggling. 'Let's at least thank the stars Robert is now an orphan as well as being an only child. If he'd come from a big family too, half of us would be sleeping in the stables, which might be apropos at Christmas but jolly chilly, I'd have thought.'

Laura wiped tears of laughter from her eyes. 'There could be complete chaos if all the children woke up to find Father Christmas in the night nursery.'

'Oh dear, what shall we do? I'd forgotten all about Father Christmas.'

'You'd forgotten? How could you have when that is the whole point of their visit?' Laura exclaimed.

Overcome with gales of laughter, the sisters were still guffawing loudly, unaware their mother, the Dowager Countess of Rothbury, was standing in the door watching them disapprovingly.

'May I ask why you're both behaving like kitchen maids in a scullery?' she asked crisply.

'Mama!' Diana jumped to her feet like a child who's been caught stealing chocolate biscuits. 'I'm so sorry. I never heard you arrive.'

'I would have thought we all made enough noise to awaken the dead,' her mother replied.

Laura was the only one who had never been scared of her mother. She rose slowly – a tall, slim and elegant figure in a dark plum-red dress, which showed off her small waist.

'Hello, Mama. You're looking very well,' she said, kissing her lightly on the cheek. 'Where are the others?'

'We're here,' chorused her three younger sisters as they came rushing into the room.

'We were checking we had all our luggage,' said Alice, sounding flustered.

'The trouble is we have far too many suitcases,' complained Flora.

'That's because we're so looking forward to dressing up for dinner every night! We haven't really done it since we left Lochlee,' added Catriona in a small voice.

Laura gave Catriona a hug and kissed her warmly. She felt particularly sorry for the youngest member of the family because she'd had to leave the castle when it was sold and, apart from attending the last ball Lady Rothbury had held before the new owners took possession, she'd gone straight from the schoolroom to a comfortable but very ordinary house. Unlike her mother and sisters, she had missed out on knowing what it was like to be a grown-up living in a grand castle that had belonged to the Fairbairn family for five hundred years.

It was all right for Alice, who had married the local parson the following year when she turned twenty, and Flora, who had made up her mind to become a teacher, but for Catriona it was staying at home, doing needlework and reading the newspapers aloud as her mother's eyesight deteriorated.

Lady Rothbury had long ago decided she would keep the

sweetest and most amenable of all her daughters at home with her as the perfect companion with which she would share her dotage. Watching her mother send Catriona off to fetch a cushion for her back made Laura sad, but Catriona seemed to relish her role of a nurse. It made her feel important and at the same time safe from the world. Laura was of the opinion that her mother shouldn't be allowed to deliberately force Catriona into spinsterhood for her personal benefit, but Diana had insisted it was what their youngest sister wanted.

At that moment they began to hear the approach of several motors, and suddenly the rest of the Fairbairn family were spilling out on to the drive, greeting each other with hugs and cries of delight. This was the first time they'd all gathered together at Cranley Court, and it was a bittersweet reunion because they no longer had Lochlee.

Diana's husband, Robert Kelso, went out to greet them all while the footmen rushed around, collecting the luggage.

'Welcome!' he said. 'How lovely to see you all.' Kissing the women on the cheek and shaking the men by the hand, he led everyone into the hall, including the eldest of the Fairbairn sisters, Lizzie, with her husband Sir Humphrey Garding and their four daughters. Beattie followed behind them with her husband Andrew Drinkwater, who had travelled all the way from London.

Always keen to show off his wealth and the only son-in-law who was 'in trade', Andrew pumped Robert's hand enthusiastically.

'Hello there, old chap. By George, this new train, the Royal Scot, is remarkable! We booked first class, of course.'

'Of course,' Robert agreed gravely, but his eyes were twinkling with amusement.

'It's the last word in luxury,' Andrew continued. 'It's only been running for a few months and the restaurant car is magnificent – not quite the Ritz, you know, but jolly good. The wine list is excellent. It was built in England in spite of its name, you know. So here we are in two ticks because I ordered three motor cars to meet us at the station in Edinburgh and bring us here.'

Robert's eyebrows rose a fraction. 'Three cars?'

'One for Beattie and I, another for Nanny, Henry, Kathleen and Camilla and then, of course, one for the luggage.'

'Of course,' Robert said gently before making a move to talk to the rest of his guests, but Andrew hadn't finished.

'It's incredible to think it's the fastest passenger express so far with Pullman-style cabins. Do you know one day it might even be possible for ordinary people to travel like that?'

'Oh, I do hope so,' Robert retorted.

The drawing room was crowded now and children were running all over the place while Burton stood in the middle of the hall keeping track of everyone's luggage, commanding the footmen to take it upstairs where Mrs Armstrong would make sure it was put in the right rooms.

Meanwhile, Jock, the six-year-old son of Georgie and her husband Shane O'Mally, was doing his best to create chaos by throwing a small cardboard aeroplane into the air again and again.

'Mind out!' Flora snapped sharply in her schoolmarm manner. 'That could hurt someone, Jock.'

Georgie, very overweight after the births of her three children, smiled indulgently. 'He's all right. He's only playing.'

'He could knock over the Dresden figurines on the mantelpiece,' warned Lizzie, inwardly thankful she'd had four girls.

'It's only a small toy,' Georgie pointed out. Unfortunately, Jock chose that moment to deliberately target Diana, hurling the aeroplane up into the air, where it crashed into the side of Diana's face, causing her to give a small shriek of shock.

'Where did that come from?' she asked.

'Your nephew is trying to kill you,' Flora retorted, turning on Georgie angrily. 'You really should keep him under control. The child is a menace.'

Shane O'Mally sauntered towards them, grinning from ear to ear. 'It's only a bit of cardboard, Flo, and he's just a kid . . .'

Jock, who was watching Diana, roared with laughter as she rubbed her cheek. Then he ran to pick up his toy from the floor but Flora was nearer and scooped it up, refusing to give it back to him.

'You're not to play with this indoors again,' she told him

firmly. 'You've hurt poor Aunt Di. Supposing it had gone into her eye?'

'You've no right to speak to my son like that,' Georgie said querulously.

Flora swiftly retaliated. 'I wouldn't have to if you'd brought him up properly.'

'Leave Georgie alone,' said Shane defensively. 'She's a first-rate mother.'

At that moment their four-year-old son, Ian, grabbed a cushion from an armchair and threw it in the direction of his eight-year-old sister, Harriet, but missed, instead knocking over a vase of flowers on a side table, soaking her.

'Bugger you!' she screamed, looking down at her wet dress.

Shane grabbed both Jock and Ian by the scruff of the neck and marched them out of the room. Then he could be heard in the hall scolding his sons in his broad Irish accent for 'making a show of me and your Mum', and telling them that he'd 'have the hide of you both if you do it again, see if I don't'.

Diana stepped forward to take control of the situation. 'Why don't we all have a cup of tea while the nannies take the children up to the day nursery,' she announced firmly. 'Burton, could you possibly . . .?' There was no need for her to continue. The butler was already standing in the doorway and he would carry out her wishes quickly and without fuss because he had an impressive instinct in what needed to be done. Quietly and calmly the children were ushered upstairs and, a few minutes later, several footmen were offering the guests refreshing cups of tea, an array of dainty cucumber sandwiches and small cakes with pink sugar icing.

'Full marks for diplomacy, Di,' whispered Laura. 'Has Georgie gone up to the nursery with Harriet?'

Diana nodded and replied in a perfect Irish accent, 'Apparently Harriet didn't want "no bleedin' nanny taking off me wet dress".'

Laura nearly choked on her tea in an effort to stop laughing. 'Is that what Harriet said?'

'Loud and clear. I think everyone except Mama heard her. I thought Burton was going to faint.'

'It's catching, too.'

Diana looked alarmed. 'What do you mean?'

'Children are notorious for copying each other. By Boxing Day they'll all be effing and blinding. We might even learn a few choice new words ourselves,' she added darkly.

'Oh, no! You don't really think so, do you? Robert will go mad.' Diana rose from her chair. 'I must go and have a word with Georgie and Shane.' As she hurried out of the room Lizzie came over to sit beside Laura.

'What is Di doing?' she asked.

Laura explained.

Lizzie shrugged. 'Yes, those children will have to be stopped if only for their own sakes. Do you remember when I said "oh my God" when I was about fifteen? Mama and Papa's faces! He told me "never to take the name of the Lord God in vain". Then I was sent to my room and not allowed to join all of you for dinner. Or for breakfast the next day!'

'Yes, I do remember. Mind you, I don't think that either Jock or Harriet knew they were swearing. That's what made it so funny. They've got the faces of angels and the tongues of gutter-snipes, I'm afraid.'

Lizzie smiled. 'It's very brave of Di to have invited the whole family for Christmas. I hope she's not going to regret it. It's the first time we've all been under the same roof since that last night at Lochlee three years ago.'

'How the time has flown,' Laura observed.

'Slower for some than for others.' Lizzie suddenly looked terribly tired, and her mouth tightened.

'What is it?' Laura asked.

'Nothing. Nothing at all.'

'Come on, Lizzie. I always know when you're trying to hide something.'

Lizzie looked at her with pain-filled eyes. 'Well, I – gosh; I don't quite know what to say.' She looked away for a moment and took a breath. And then, in a low voice, she whispered, 'I've fallen in love with someone. He's . . . he's the most wonderful young man.' She stopped instantly, regretting her use of the word 'young'.

Laura pounced on it like a cat catching a mouse. 'How old is he?'

Lizzie blushed and refused to meet her sister's eye.

'Lizzie?'

'Twenty-three. Humphrey has no idea, of course.'

'But your girls?' Laura protested in a horrified undertone. 'What about them?'

Lizzie spoke bitterly. 'Having children doesn't make one immune to falling in love.'

Laura sat in silent bewilderment. Of all the sisters, Lizzie was the last one she'd have expected to behave like this. Furthermore, Humphrey was one of the nicest men she'd ever met: kind, humorous, and able to give his family a very comfortable existence in a lovely house in London.

'How old is Margaret now?' she asked.

Lizzie looked pained. 'She's ten and Isabel is eight.'

Laura nodded. 'Then Rose must be sixteen and Emma seventeen.' She paused before saying coldly, 'Shouldn't you be looking out for suitable young men for them, instead of for yourself?'

Tears sprang to Lizzie's hazel eyes.

'I simply couldn't resist Justin,' she said brokenly as she averted her face to hide her tears. 'I love Humphrey; he's a dear man! But when I met Justin I realized I'd never been in love before. I've never felt like this before, and I thought . . .' She paused before continuing in a rush of words, 'I suddenly realized this was my last chance of really understanding what being in love actually meant. I can't tell you how glorious it is when . . .' Her voice faded with emotion.

'For heaven's sake, Lizzie, you're forty now. In August you'll be forty-one. You simply can't let yourself get carried away by this infatuation. Think of your wonderful husband! And what would your girls say? It will harm their future chances of making good marriages. They'll be notorious! Known as the children of a woman who had a love affair with a man young enough to be her son . . . You've got to stop this folly right away.'

'Keep your voice down,' Lizzie whispered fiercely.

Laura leaned back in her chair so she could cast her eyes casually around the room. Humphrey was deep in conversation with Robert and Andrew at the far end of the room and

Beattie, Alice, Catriona and Flora were seated in a circle, chatting brightly to each other and laughing a lot. Laura wished with all her heart that she were a part of their happy group instead of being burdened by Lizzie's dreadful secret.

At that moment Georgie and Shane came back into the room with Diana, who was smiling broadly.

'That's the young'uns sorted out,' Shane announced. 'They've been taken to look at the horses. That'll keep them quiet for a bit.'

Lizzie, having unburdened herself, smiled serenely while Laura took a deep breath and wished that life wasn't so complicated. For the past three years she'd struggled to get over her husband's alcoholism that had eventually led to their bankruptcy, leaving their six-year-old daughter and her with nothing but the clothes on their backs as he was once again hospitalized. Their home and all their possessions had gone. If it hadn't been for Diana they'd have literally been on the streets. When she'd borrowed the money to start her dressmaking business, once again Laura had faced a heart-breaking struggle to make ends meet. There were nights when she'd lain awake with sheer hunger. She feared the mail every day, terrified that it might be a final demand to pay her gas or electricity bill, and enough money had to be put aside for the rent of their little two-room flat, which had to be in an area of Edinburgh where her clients would be willing to come for fittings.

It had been so different when she'd started her business before her marriage to Walter. She had only herself to think about and only herself to feed. Now she had Caroline, who showed great promise as a ballet dancer. Her father lived with his sister now and Caroline adored him. Laura had loved him once but his addiction had worn it away – all she felt now was a kind of pity and sadness at the loss of the kind and loving man he used to be. Alcoholism had obliterated a once noble soldier, husband and father.

It had been a hard struggle to get back on her feet but she'd managed; all she wanted now was to be able to give Caroline a good education and training in ballet.

At that moment Laura was struck by the full realization that

Lizzie was in danger of risking everything in her foolish pursuit of sexual gratification. Sir Humphrey Garding was a warm and delightful man with wealth, a beautiful country house and the means to provide Lizzie and their four daughters with a life of quiet elegance.

Laura turned back to look at Lizzie and felt like shaking some sense into her. She had to be stopped at all costs.

Up in the bedrooms and dressing rooms of Cranley Court, all the guests were changing for dinner, assisted by their maids and valets, while on the top floor a score of nannies and nursery maids were giving the little ones their supper before putting them to bed.

'Are you all right, old girl?' asked Humphrey, wandering into Lizzie's room.

'Why shouldn't I be?' she responded tartly. She was sitting at the dressing table, staring at her reflection.

'You seemed put out when you were talking to Laura,' he replied mildly. 'Is she all right? Are you worried about her?'

Lizzie looked surprised. 'Laura's always all right. God knows how she manages. I suppose she's very strong.'

'To have survived what she's been through, she'd have to be.' He laid his hand affectionately on her pale bare shoulder. 'I never worry about her,' he added quietly.

Lizzie rose quickly to avoid his caress. 'Let's go downstairs. I hope Diana's giving us all champagne before dinner.' She swept out of room, her beauty and elegance undiminished by age. 'Come along, Humphrey.' She spoke impatiently. 'The others are probably in the drawing room by now.'

He followed her slowly. Something was wrong and he was determined to find out what troubled her.

Up in the nursery, Laura, who had already changed into a rich satin dinner dress in dark plum red, trimmed with matching lace, was reading a bedtime story to Caroline, the only mother among all of her sisters to do so.

'How long are we staying here, Muzzie?' the child asked.

'For six days. Isn't that lovely?'

'I wished we lived here. Aunt Di would let us, wouldn't she?'

'It wouldn't be fair if we did, darling. It wouldn't be right to sponge off her and Uncle Robert. And we're all right on our own, aren't we? The flat's cosy and it's nice to be in the centre of Edinburgh. You'd miss your ballet classes, wouldn't you?'

Caroline lay still, frowning. 'If we can't live here why can't we live with Papa and Aunt Rowena? Papa wants us to be with him and she's got a nice house.'

Laura rose. 'How would I make money if we lived in the country? I have to be in Edinburgh.' She bent over her daughter and stroked her face tenderly. 'Now go to sleep. I must go and help your grandmama go down to dinner.' She stooped to kiss Caroline but the child buried her head in the pillow. 'We always have to do what you want,' she said rudely.

Laura recoiled at her daughter's words, stung, and stood silently over her for a moment before turning and slowly making her way down to collect her mother.

Lady Rothbury had aged greatly since she'd been forced to leave Lochlee, largely because of the crushing death duties that had been incurred by the deaths of Lord Rothbury and his two heirs, Freddie and her beloved younger son, Henry. After five hundred years of prosperity, the castle and hundreds of acres had been sold, and although the nearby manse was comfortable, she'd never recovered from the shock and the grief.

'There you are, dear,' she greeted Laura with a brief kiss on the cheek. 'I thought you might have forgotten you'd promised to take me down.'

'How could I possibly forget?' Laura asked, forcing herself to sound cheerful, although she still felt hurt by Caroline's attitude. 'It's so lovely we're all together for Christmas, isn't it? Goodness knows how Di has managed to fit us all in.'

Lady Rothbury nodded sagely. 'She made a very good marriage, that's how.'

Laura didn't reply as she took her mother's arm to help her down the wide, oak, red-carpeted staircase. In the hall below, Beattie and Andrew were talking to Georgie and Shane, and through the open drawing-room door all they could hear was a babble of voices and excited laughter from Catriona and Flora.

'They all sound very happy,' Lady Rothbury remarked indulgently.

At that moment Lizzie and Humphrey emerged from the library. They were both tight-lipped and she looked flushed and angry. Laura's heart sank. Maybe this wasn't going to be the congenial family gathering she'd imagined.

It was clear even to the staff that Sir Humphrey and Lady Elizabeth Garding had 'had words'.

'Is anything wrong, dearest?' Diana whispered to Lizzie as they all trooped into the candlelit dining room, where the long mahogany table was laid with magnificent silver and crystal glasses and garlands of holly decorated with scarlet satin ribbons.

Lizzie looked at her sharply. 'What has Laura said to you?'

Diana blinked, surprised. 'Nothing. I just thought you looked upset. I've placed you between Robert and Andrew. Is that all right?'

'Perfectly fine.'

Diana looked at her doubtfully, watching Lizzie force a hard, cold smile, although her eyes were over-bright.

'Get a move on, you two,' said Georgie as she followed them into the imposing dining room, where up to thirty guests could be seated.

There were small cards bearing the name of each guest at every place setting so everyone was quickly and smoothly seated. Laura was delighted to find her host on her left side and Humphrey on her right. They were her two favourite brothers-in-law and she flashed Diana a grateful smile. Her sister grinned back and slightly raised one eyebrow as she gently tilted her head towards the two men she was sitting between. To keep the numbers even she'd invited the local mayor and a retired doctor, both in their seventies. Laura tried to repress a giggle. Diana knew exactly how to do the right thing and she admired that very much. Glancing around the table she saw that their mother was seated between two charming men of her generation, one a bachelor and the other a widower, and that Flora was next to a professor of science, while Catriona discovered that the young man on her right was a violinist in a big orchestra. This, Laura assured herself, was going to be the best Christmas of her life.

At the top of the house Caroline lay in the darkness of one of the small bedrooms next to the night nursery, aware of the snuffling and sighing of some of her cousins as they fell asleep. Normally she slept in her mother's room, but Aunt Di had insisted Muzzie must have one of the grand suites on the first floor with its carved four-poster bed and beautiful oyster silk hangings.

'You need a good rest, Laura,' she'd heard Aunt Di say. 'I've given orders that you're to have breakfast in bed. And if you appear downstairs before noon I'll send you right back to bed again!' Then Caroline heard her mother laughing happily, something she seldom did when they were at home.

A deep pang of jealousy arose in Caroline's chest. Why should she have to share an ugly, stuffy little room with Aunt Lizzie's and Aunt Beattie's little girls and the badly behaved Harriet?

Rage flowed through her veins like poison and she kicked the foot of her bed viscously. Why didn't she live in a beautiful big house? It wasn't fair. That was the constant mantra that filled her mind. It wasn't fair. Why didn't she have expensive shoes like all the other girls? Why didn't she have more clothes? Bought at an expensive shop, instead of things made by Muzzie?

All her cousins had nicer lives than she did and it was so unfair. Round and round her bitter grievances went in her head, slowly causing her to cry quietly, the sobs busting forth from her throat with an ugly sound.

'Are you all right, Caroline?'

She recognized the voice of Aunt Lizzie's prettiest daughter, Margaret.

Caroline lay still in the darkness, not answering. She particularly hated Margaret, who was a year older. She had a sunny disposition, was liked by everyone and was her grandmother's favourite – everyone's favourite. Caroline was filled with thoughts of revenge. One day she'd show Margaret who was really the prettiest, the best dressed and the most popular, and she'd make sure that Margaret would feel as unhappy as she felt at this moment.

On the floor below, both Laura and Lizzie slept fitfully. Laura tossed and turned, worried about Lizzie and what she'd confessed, and Lizzie lay awake, unable to stop counting the days until she could see Justin again. God, she loved him so much and she wanted him so desperately. She'd never felt like this before, and while she was deeply fond of Humphrey, her feelings for Justin were altogether different. She was burning up with desire, playing over in her mind that first time that he'd kissed her and she'd thought for a moment that she might faint. Such passion could not be denied. Justin loved her as much as she loved him and, lying beside Humphrey, she knew she had to leave him. When was another matter. She didn't want to think about it yet. All she wanted was to get through this family Christmas.

Justin had no ties, no responsibilities and he was a popular guest at many homes. Would he meet someone else over Christmas? An attractive woman – younger, much younger than her? He'd laughingly admitted that his mother was looking for a suitable bride for him. Every time Lizzie thought about it her heart turned to ice and she felt sick with misery. She realized with anguish that her eldest daughter Emma would, at seventeen, be a more suitable bride for a man of twenty-three. It was madness to even countenance the notion that they could run away together and live happily ever after. But she simply couldn't stop herself from dreaming about him . . . His strong, young thighs made her weak with desire. The thought of his smooth hands, not freckled and lined like Humphrey's, made her long for Justin's caresses. He was an Adonis compared to her middle-aged husband, with his thinning hair and paunch; a good man, no doubt, but beside this passionate youth he was a tired old man. Her passion for him was long spent.

How could she resist Justin's ardent kisses, which sent shockwaves through her body? How could she turn a deaf ear to his tender words of love? Lizzie realized that if she had resisted the powerful rush of passion on that first occasion, when he'd been desperate to possess her, she might have died without ever experiencing real love.

Turning over carefully in bed so as not to awaken Humphrey, she lay on her stomach, pressing herself against the hard mattress and wishing with all her heart she was with Justin.

The following day belonged to the children, who awoke at dawn and proceeded to continue opening their presents for the rest of the day.

'Children weren't indulged like this in my day,' Lady Rothbury observed tartly.

'It only happens once a year,' Diana said soothingly, 'and it is a wonderful opportunity for all of us to get together.'

Laura, who was sitting next to her mother, looked anxious. 'I have a terrible feeling that this is the last time we'll all be together,' she murmured quietly.

Lady Rothbury looked at her sharply. 'Now don't go spoiling everything with your "second sight"! You probably have a premonition that I'll be dead by this time next year . . . well, if I am, I am, and the rest of you will have to get on with things,' she stated matter-of-factly.

Laura looked shocked. 'My feelings aren't about you at all, Mama. I have a feeling . . . like the one I had before the Boer War? In eighteen . . . ?'

'Eighteen ninety-nine,' Lady Rothbury said immediately, her face grave.

'I knew it was going to happen.' Laura's voice faltered. 'I . . . I knew Henry would never come back . . .'

'Killed on the last day of the war.' Diana shuddered at the memory of their handsome young brother setting off with excitement to fight the Boers.

'I feel now what I felt then,' said Laura. 'There couldn't be another war so soon, could there?'

Robert, who was sitting nearby, commented gravely, 'Laura isn't speaking from second sight. The unrest all over Europe is mounting and at any time the most serious war the world has ever known will involve all of us. Every man, woman and child. The situation couldn't be more serious.'

Diana looked at her husband, her expression anxious. 'Is it really as bad as that?' she asked.

'I don't want to sound gloomy,' Robert said carefully. 'Not today.' He looked at his wife's frightened face and forced a hard smile. 'It could be worse. Much, much worse.'

Two

Caroline stomped into her mother's bedroom at dawn with the air of an aggrieved five-year-old child.

'Wake up, Muzzie,' she demanded impatiently.

Laura awoke with a start. A damp grey day was seeping through a gap in the curtains, making her heart sink. Not another day in this damned house, she reflected. How she hated being here. How she longed to go back to sleep and the joy of oblivion. She wished they were back in their Edinburgh flat, but every few months she felt obligated to take the child to spend some time with her father, who lived with his widowed sister, Rowena. 'What's the matter?' she asked drowsily.

'I don't want to go home tomorrow.' Caroline pouted like a toddler. And her eyes, so dark and button bright, like her father's, glinted balefully at Laura. 'I hardly ever see Dada. Why can't we see him more often? Aunt Rowena wouldn't mind if we stayed just for a few more days. I don't want to go back to that horrible little flat.'

Laura sat up in bed and spoke gently but firmly. 'Darling, I have work to do. We've already been here for five days and I have customers coming to see me tomorrow. I'm afraid I can't stay away because we need the money.'

Caroline stamped her foot. 'It's not fair. It's always work, work, work. You use it as an excuse when you don't want to do something. Especially if it's something that I want to do. Dada always has time for me but you never do.'

Laura hid her hurt and anger to avoid a scene but it was a hard pill to swallow. The last thing she needed was a contretemps in front of Walter and Rowena but the way Caroline twisted the facts and showed not a trace of gratitude was like a knife through her heart.

The bedroom door slammed and Laura was alone again with

tears pouring down her cheeks. There was no doubt that Caroline worshipped her father and she'd been very careful never to say anything critical about him. But surely the child realized that she, her mother, worked a twelve-hour day so that Caroline had a chance of following her dreams and becoming a leading ballet dancer? She wondered what the problem was. Did she indulge her and spoil her too much? Did she get her own way too often? Caroline had enjoyed a wonderful Christmas with Di, and they'd travelled to Rowena's house in good time to spend New Year's Eve with her father. Instead of being happy Caroline had never stopped grumbling that her cousins had everything in life and she had nothing. It had made Laura realize that no matter how hard she worked or what she did, nothing was ever going to match Caroline's expectations. Nothing was ever as good as she'd hoped. No dress would ever be pretty enough. No party she was invited to would ever be as much fun as she thought it would. No present would ever be what she really wanted. Life would never be what she'd hoped for, Laura realized with growing concern. If her father were to inherit a fortune from an elderly relative it still wouldn't be enough to satisfy Caroline.

Drying her eyes, Laura started to pack. The sooner they got home the better. Caroline would immediately fret that their flat was too small, too cold or too hot, that she hated the neighbourhood – but it couldn't be helped. Life could be hard but Laura had no intention of sponging off her rich sisters.

At that moment there was a knock on her bedroom door.

'Come in!' Guessing it was Rowena, she forced herself to sound cheerful.

Rowena came into the room and closed the door quietly behind her. She spoke in hushed tones. 'Caroline has asked if you and she can stay for a few more days. Walter told her that it would be fine.'

'That's very naughty of her,' Laura replied firmly. 'I've already told her I have to get back to Edinburgh because I have customers coming to see me.' She sighed. 'How typical of Walter to tell her we could stay on.'

Rowena shrugged. 'You know what he's like. He's incapable of saying "no" to anyone or anything.'

'How true. I'll finish packing and then we'll be off.'

Downstairs in the breakfast room, Caroline was hanging on to Walter's arm, crying petulantly, 'It's not fair. I want to stay with you, Dada! Why can't I live with you? Why can't I stay with you for ever and ever?'

'Yes, well, maybe when you're a bit bigger,' Walter replied weakly.

'Can I then? I hate living with Muzzie. I'm never allowed to do anything I want. She's really horrible to me.'

Laura walked into the room at that moment and she pretended she hadn't overheard what had been said.

'Laura, do you really have to leave today?' Walter asked.

'You know perfectly well that I have to get back to work,' she said determinedly. 'Rowena and I worked out the dates long ago, and I've explained to Caroline that work comes before pleasure.'

Their daughter gave a little pirouette and said smugly, 'Dada has just told me that I can stay here whenever I want when I'm bigger.'

Rowena looked up sharply but said nothing. Knowing Caroline was trying to get a rise out of her, Laura also remained silent. The sooner they got home the better, she reflected.

Three

Laura settled down to work again with an enormous sense of relief. Caroline was back at school and ballet classes, which she loved, and her discontent had seemed to fade once she was back in their old routine. It was obvious to Laura that staying with their well-off relations had unsettled Caroline. How could they not?

January was a quiet month in her business, apart from a few rich customers who always wanted new gowns to wear to big social occasions.

This was when Laura started to plan ahead for the coming year, attempting to predict the changing fashions. By the end of the month she'd be ordering suitable fabrics for dresses, jackets and lightweight coats.

What would the style be? She loved designing more than anything; she had always had dreams of being a fashion designer with a dozen young women doing the actual cutting, fitting and stitching. She'd heard that one day sewing machines would be electric and so much quicker. Meanwhile, she had to slog away and be thankful that garments no longer had to be made entirely by hand.

She decided that after a freezing, icy winter, no one was going to want garments made of wool, tweed or velvet, or fur-trimmed brocade in rich colours. The materials should echo the soft loveliness of spring. Orders for fabric must be given to the manufacturers in good time and she must be able to provide a wide choice, to avoid the embarrassment of two of her ladies turning up at a function in the same material.

How refreshing it would be to create gowns of delicate fabric, and if they were the pastel shade of spring flowers that would be *de rigueur*. Now she visualized satin that was the colour of primroses and silk in that tender pink of a hyacinth.

Then there was the blue of bluebells. In her mind's eye she could see a ball gown in chiffon, drifting and fluttering as the wearer moved. The ideas were coming thick and fast now and she reached for her box of pencils and her pad of artists' paper. With growing excitement, she started sketching. This was the part she enjoyed the most. A few minutes later she'd drawn a dress of stylish but restrained elegance – perfect for her younger customers who could still show their arms and necklines. A few minutes later she'd completed a drawing for the older ladies, with long sleeves and a neckline softened by frills.

Smiling to herself, Laura continued to design more dresses, skirts, pretty blouses and well-cut coats and jackets. The cut was of paramount importance, along with the quality of the material. She particularly liked cutting on the cross, so that a garment appeared moulded to the body.

That night when Caroline was asleep in the little room they shared, she made a list of women who had been recommended to go to her. From the business point of view, the next twelve months looked highly profitable. Two of her young customers were getting married and their mothers would no doubt need splendid outfits. There would likely be bridesmaids to be dressed, not to mention the bridal gown and veil.

It was also time she began to charge just a little bit more. Industrialists' wives now wanted to dress like the gentry. They certainly had the money but it was the cachet of going to Lady Laura, daughter of an earl that really counted, because she had such good taste.

Even though the future looked very good, with enough income to keep Caroline at her ballet classes, there still lurked at the back of Laura's mind a dark shadow of fear and uncertainty. She'd learned long ago that nothing in life could be depended on.

The next morning a letter from Lizzie arrived, and Laura slipped it into her handbag until she'd taken Caroline to school. The child was so inquisitive and questioned her all the time about everything and anything. Laura knew it was because of the utter shock she must have felt on the day Walter was declared bankrupt, when they had helplessly watched as the bailiffs ordered the men to fill their lorry with the entire contents of their beautiful home. To her dying day she would remember the expression of incomprehension and unhappiness when Caroline saw her favourite toys being tossed casually away.

Lizzie and Beattie had told her she was spoiling Caroline, but Laura felt a great need to make up to Caroline all that she'd lost. Perhaps she was a bit spoilt, but they hadn't seen the desolate look in her eyes or the droop of her mouth on the day she had lost her home and virtually her father too.

Sitting down when she was alone, Laura ripped open the envelope and read Lizzie's letter.

> *Dearest Laura,*
>
> *I'm in a terrible state and I don't know what to do. Humphrey picked up a book I was reading and he found a letter from Justin between the pages. All he said was 'enjoying the book?' but he knows now. Justin wants me to run away with him and he's given me a month to make up my mind. I desperately want to go with him and a part of me feels that I'll fall apart if I don't take this chance. I love him so much but I'm frightened of the future, too . . . I've never felt like this before over any man and I can't sleep at night for thinking about him. Laura, my darling sister, advise me. Dare I risk everything and go?*
>
> *Love,*
> *Lizzie*

Laura read it several times, committing it to memory before going into her small kitchen, reaching for a box of matches and setting fire to it over the sink. Then she turned on the taps and the fragments of black paper disappeared down the drain. Whatever happened, Caroline must have no knowledge of this family crisis.

That night, she wrote a long and sympathetic letter to her sister, where she tried to point out the pros and cons of what she was considering. She gently suggested:

> *I think you and Humphrey should go for a romantic holiday. Just the two of you. Tell him you've always wanted to visit Venice. Tell him you're exhausted and you'd love it if you could*

*be alone together without the constant chatter of your daughters,
and running the house. I think it's only fair to try and save
your marriage. Try and think of it as a second honeymoon . . .*

The next morning she posted the letter and prayed Lizzie
would see sense. Humphrey was a good, kind man and he didn't
deserve the heartbreak of being deserted for someone twenty
years younger. More importantly, Margaret, Isabel, Rose and
Emma should never have to suffer the grief and the scandal of
having a mother with a bad reputation.

'That should do the trick,' Laura muttered under her breath
as she dropped her reply into the letterbox.

London, 1914

It looked like a large private house in Hans Place but it was
a private hotel. Very private. Lizzie came out of the side
entrance of Harrods and looked both ways before she crossed
the street. Making sure there was no one she knew around,
she hurried over to the entrance of the hotel, where the door
opened as if by magic. Slipping inside she heard the concierge
say, 'Mr Hammond is in room seven, madam.'

'Thank you,' Lizzie replied under her breath, thanking God
that Justin was there already.

Hurrying along the now-familiar corridor that led to room
seven, her heart was thumping with excitement and nerves.

As if he sensed her imminent arrival, the door opened and
a moment later she was in his arms as he held her close. Then
he kissed her with such passion she felt weak. Leading her to
the large bed, he pulled her down beside him.

'My darling one,' he whispered softly as he gently unbut-
toned her coat. Lizzie arched her back, slipping off her buckled
shoes. Justin lingered over undressing her, and the longer he
took the more feverishly she desired him. Groaning with
longing, she reached out for him and with lightning speed he
tore off his own clothes. Then, naked, he lay down beside her,
whispering words of love.

'I love you too,' she murmured, stroking his strong, young
body. It flashed through her mind that whatever the future

held he belonged to her in this moment, body, mind and soul, and she would remember it for the rest of her life. Their mingled cries of passion rose to a crescendo and then they lay, sated and spent.

'Have you decided what to do?' he asked eventually.

Lizzie propped herself up on her elbow and looked beseechingly into Justin's face. 'How can I leave my family?' she asked despairingly. 'I love you with all my heart, and of course I want to spend the rest of my life with you. But I have a duty to stay and look after my daughters . . .' She buried her face in his chest and murmured, 'Can't we continue to meet secretly?'

Justin averted his face to hide his disappointment. 'I'm an all or nothing sort of man. This isn't fair on Humphrey or your family. I want to marry you and have you bear my children . . .' His voice broke and he got up from the bed and started dressing hurriedly.

Lizzie sat up on the bed, looking slightly alarmed. 'Give me a little longer, darling. I love you so much. I'm sure we can work out something . . .'

Justin bent over her to kiss her on the mouth: a long, lingering kiss. And then, without a word, he hurried from the room, closing the door behind him, leaving Lizzie feeling shocked. She'd never seen him so emotional before. Getting dressed quickly she left the hotel just as another, rather tarty-looking woman entered the lobby. Giving Lizzie a knowing look she asked the concierge boldly, 'Is it room twelve as usual?'

He nodded and, startled by the woman's cockney accent, Lizzie realized this hotel was where men met their mistresses. With flaming cheeks she hurried out of the building, appalled that Justin had chosen such a place to meet her. Once in the safety of Harrods, she found herself wandering from department to department, confused and troubled. Where could they meet in future? Should she rent a little flat?

When she returned to their home in Kensington, she was surprised to see a telegram on the hall table addressed to her. Wondering if her mother had been taken ill, or whether one of her sisters was trying to alert her urgently, she ripped open the envelope, then collapsed to her knees, crying bitterly.

Edinburgh, 1914

Laura recognized Lizzie's handwriting and quickly slipped her letter into her handbag before Caroline saw it. Once she was alone she opened the envelope with trepidation. Her advice to Lizzie had been quite stern and this was probably a missive telling her to mind her own business, but on the contrary the letter filled her with sympathy.

I'm absolutely heartbroken and don't know what to do. I'm in bed and Humphrey and the girls think I'm ill and having a breakdown because I can't stop crying. The doctor has given me something but it's not really working. I met Justin last week and I thought everything between us was all right. I told him that I didn't think I could abandon Humphrey and the girls, but I suggested that we continue to see each other as we had been doing. I could see he was upset and he said he wanted to marry me and have children by me, but he's said that before. Then he just left! When I got home there was a telegram for me. It was from him, saying he'd joined the army because we'd soon be at war. That was all. No goodbye. I was so shocked I collapsed on the hall floor. One minute we're in heaven together and then I tell him I can't leave Humphrey . . . and he's gone. For ever. I've tried to get hold of him but it's as though he's vanished! What am I to do now? I fear I'll never get over this terrible blow. Please, Laura, write back to me when you can. I'm despairing.

Laura felt a mixture of sorrow and relief for Lizzie, who was obviously devastated. She remembered the fearful pain of her own loss when Rory had been killed. At least Lizzie had known the joy of lovemaking with the man of her dreams. That was something she knew she would regret all her life. She'd been seventeen at the time and her mother had instructed all her daughters that they must remain virgins until their wedding night.

Justin had done the right and noble thing by removing himself from Lizzie's life, and for that Laura felt grateful. A clean cut instead of a long-drawn-out farewell was for the best. This way there was no going back. Hundreds of young men were joining the army and the Fleet Air Arm because they knew war was inevitable, and Justin had killed two birds with one stone by signing up and ending the affair.

Four

Cranley Court, June 1914

Laura felt an icy rush of alarm and her heart seemed to miss a beat.

'Oh my God,' she murmured aloud as she gazed at the newspaper headline.

'What is it?' Diana asked as she came down the staircase. Every morning the butler arranged the newspapers with precision on the hall table as if they were ornamental and not to be touched.

Laura and Caroline were spending the weekend with Diana, where, as always, the atmosphere was serene and the setting luxurious.

'Oh my God,' Diana echoed her sister's words as she saw the headline of the *Daily Telegraph*. 'This will lead to trouble.' The two women looked at each other as if they couldn't believe their eyes.

'Isn't this terrible? This could lead to war.' Laura's gaze was glued to the headline.

'"Crown Prince Franz-Ferdinand of Austria and his wife were assassinated yesterday as they watched a military parade in Sarajevo . . ."' Diana read aloud. 'This is what Robert feared at Christmas. Do you remember?'

'I remember very well. I had a feeling the New Year was going to be troublesome,' Laura said sadly.

'Perhaps it will blow over. Foreigners are so excitable,' Diana remarked as she led the way into the breakfast room. 'But I've always said the Queen made a big mistake in getting each of her daughters married off to crown heads. Why didn't she let them marry members of the British aristocracy? God knows, there are quite a few dukes and marquises who would have fitted the bill perfectly.'

Laura looked at Diana scornfully. 'Would any of them want

the job? I can't think of anything worse. All that protocol and bowing and scraping.'

Later that day, as they walked in the vast grounds of Cranley Court accompanied by Bruno and Augustus, Diana's two Labradors, she turned to Laura and asked, 'Have you heard from Lizzie recently?'

Laura hesitated before answering and so Diana continued hurriedly, 'I know about Justin.'

'You do? Thank heaven's for that. The last I heard was that Justin had joined up.'

Diana nodded. 'Poor Lizzie. It must have been a terrible shock.'

'Yes, but it was for the best. It wasn't fair on Humphrey or their girls. And just think of the scandal. The tabloids would have gone to town about a middle-aged earl's daughter running off with someone young enough to be her son. It would have ruined her daughters' lives. I really don't know what she was thinking to begin with.'

'You're not being very sympathetic, Laura,' Diana said gently.

'What do you mean? Why should Humphrey and those beautiful girls suffer so Lizzie can enjoy some brief fling? I think she was being terribly selfish. I told her she had to think about them and not just herself.'

Diana looked slightly shocked. 'You sound like Mama,' she observed. 'Did you also refer to hellfire and all that?'

'Don't be silly, Di. This is no laughing matter.'

Diana was silent for a moment then looked straight into Laura face. Then she asked, 'Have you ever been passionately in love?'

Laura's pale skin flushed red and her hazel eyes brimmed with sudden tears. 'Yes, I have,' she shot back furiously. 'You seem to forget that the love of my life was Rory Drummond, and he was killed before we were able to get married. But I don't feel the need to bore everyone about it.' Her voice broke.

Diana immediately put her arm around her sister's shoulders. 'I didn't mean to upset you, dearest. Of course I remember that tragedy, but I was only twelve then and Beattie and Georgie and I were kept in the schoolroom most of the time. It was

Lizzie who was there for you at that time. She even slept in your room.'

Laura took a lace-edged handkerchief out of her pocket. 'You think I'm being too harsh with Lizzie?'

'I know you too well to think that. I realized you're trying to prevent Lizzie from ruining her life and bringing misery upon her family but when you fall desperately and madly in love with someone it's the hardest thing in the world to give them up.' Diana's eyes were over-bright and her lips trembled.

Laura looked at her in astonishment. 'You sound as if . . .?'

Diana nodded quickly and pulled herself together. 'I fell in love three or four years ago. He lived very near here and he asked me to go to London with him. He was a lawyer and very ambitious. He had money, a wonderful sense of humour . . .' Her voice trailed off.

'Did Robert know what was going on?'

'Absolutely not. We couldn't see much of each other but when we did . . .'

'Did you . . . you know?'

Diana nodded. 'Yes, we did, and it was wonderful.'

'My word! Aren't you a dark horse!' There was a note of admiration in Laura's voice.

'I had to be strong. I had Robert and the children to think about. I told Lizzie she had to be strong, too. I just hope that between us Lizzie will recover.'

Robert was very quiet at lunch that day.

'Are you all right, darling?' Diana inquired.

He looked back at her with tired eyes. 'How can any of us be all right now that war looks inevitable?' he replied. 'The assassination of Franz-Ferdinand is just what I feared. What's the date today?'

'June the twenty-eighth,' Laura replied promptly.

Robert nodded sombrely. 'I'll bet you anything you like that this will lead Great Britain into war by the beginning of August, or possibly even sooner.'

The serious tone in which he spoke startled both his wife and Laura.

'What makes you say that?' Diana said, looking shocked.

He shrugged his shoulders. 'To begin with, I wouldn't be surprised if Germany sides with Austria and Hungary, who will soon have fallen out with Serbia. And then Russia will get involved, and so it goes on until we are forced into it with France, against Germany. It's what is known as the Domino Effect.'

The two women looked at him in horror and Diana asked, 'Why do you think this, Robert?'

'My cousin, Mark Kelso, works in the Foreign Office. Whitehall has suspected for some months that something like this assassination would kick-off something that would be unstoppable. Before you know it Britain will succumb, and so will Australia and Canada, whether they want to or not.'

There was a stunned silence in the room.

'I had no idea things were so serious,' said Diana, looking stricken. The Boer War had been bad enough – their younger brother Henry had been tragically killed. This conflict however, sounded as if most of the world was going to be involved.

'Nothing will ever be the same again,' Robert warned them. 'But Great Britain will survive. We always do.'

Five

The carnage of war was at its peak, and Laura could no longer bear to read the newspapers. Every hour of every day, hundreds of young men were being killed. Those who were brought back to England were so terribly injured or shell-shocked that they would never recover, their memories of watching their fellow soldiers being slain as they charged forwards from the meagre protection of the trenches haunting them for ever.

'How can this be happening in a civilized world?' Laura asked herself in despair.

As Robert had predicted, Canadian and Australian soldiers would come to help the mother country, and they had by the thousand. What made matters worse was that there was no end to the sacrifice they had made.

Beattie's husband Andrew had joined the cavalry and Georgie's husband, Shane had volunteered and become a gunner, although he was Irish and would never have been conscripted. Due to his poor eyesight, Robert was exempt from service, and so he and Diana had turned Cranley Court into a convalescent home for the most seriously wounded in the hope that they would benefit from the peace and beauty of Scotland.

Meanwhile, Laura was struggling to make money. None of her customers, even the wealthiest ones, were entertaining, and therefore there was no demand for beautiful clothes. Mostly they came to ask Laura for black clothes of mourning.

Sometimes Laura had to fight back her own tears when a heartbroken young woman came to ask her for black clothes. It reminded her of Queen Victoria's death, when she had rushed to buy all the black fabric she could before the suppliers had run out. That had been different, though. The Queen had been an old lady, but now the dead were as young as eighteen; killed before they were grown men.

When a letter arrived from Lizzie, Laura immediately knew what had happened. The sisters were so close that she didn't have to open the envelope. Her first feeling was acute sadness, and then she hoped that Humphrey was showing compassion and forgiveness. 'Oh, God. Poor Lizzie,' she murmured aloud as she tore open the letter.

'I can't believe it, my darling, but Justin is no more . . .' There was no doubt that Lizzie had got herself into an impossible situation but this was the cruellest blow. This could break her spirit. Laura immediately went to her desk to write a letter of condolence. But as she agonized over what to write, she suddenly decided that it wasn't enough.

Late that afternoon when Caroline came home from school Laura told her, 'I've got a surprise for you.'

Caroline's face lit up. 'What is it?'

'I've arranged for you to stay for a few days with your dada. Aunt Rowena has to come up to Edinburgh tomorrow to see the dentist and she's promised to take you home with her and then bring you back here next Tuesday. Isn't that lovely?'

'What are you doing then? Why aren't you going to stay with Dada too?'

'I'm going to London for a few days.'

Caroline's face fell. 'But I want to go London too. I've never been to London. Why can't I go with you?' she demanded angrily.

'It's because Aunt Lizzie isn't well, and—'

'What's the matter with her? Why do you want to go if she's ill? You know I've always wanted to go to London.' Caroline stuck out her bottom lip like a petulant baby.

'Stop this nonsense at once, Caroline.' Laura spoke firmly. 'I'm not going for the fun of it. Aunt Lizzie needs me and that's that. You always go on about not seeing enough of Dada, and you'll have him all to yourself, which – God knows – you never stop badgering me about.'

'No, I won't. Aunt Rowena will be there,' Caroline said sulkily.

Laura turned away. 'I've told your headmistress you'll be returning to school on Wednesday. Let's go and do your packing. Aunt Rowena is picking you up tomorrow at eleven o'clock.'

Caroline shrugged but there was a glimmer of a smile on her face at the thought of seeing her father.

Laura travelled to London by train. There was no way she could afford to go first class so she sat throughout the night in a second-class carriage, unable to sleep because a baby belonging to a young woman cried on and off the whole way. At one point Laura walked along the corridor looking for a spare seat but the train was packed. By the time they steamed into King's Cross Station Laura felt cold and stiff as she carefully stepped on to the platform. Carrying her suitcase, which suddenly felt very heavy, she was startled to hear her name being called.

'Laura? Laura!'

She looked around and was shocked to see a familiar face struggling to get to her through the crowds heading for the exit.

'Humphrey!'

'Hello, my dear.' He kissed her on the cheek and grabbed her suitcase. 'I've got a car to drop you off at Cornwall Gardens but then I've got to get to work at the War Office. Sadly I'm too old for active service so I'm stuck behind a bloody desk all day.'

Laura smiled warmly. 'It's so kind of you to meet me.'

'Nonsense, my dear. It's good of you to come to see Lizzie. The poor old girl needs cheering up.'

'It's the least I could do,' she replied quietly. It was obvious he knew about Justin but it would be unseemly to mention it now or in the future.

'How is Caroline?' he asked when they were seated in the Rolls-Royce.

'Very well, thank you. She's spending a few days with her father, which she'll enjoy.'

Humphrey nodded. 'How is Walter these days?'

'He seems to have stopped drinking but his health is frail. He nearly died when he was declared bankrupt and his liver has never worked the same again.'

'I know. That was all ghastly,' Humphrey said sympathetically. 'You Fairbairn girls are remarkable, though. You picked yourself up and look how well you've done! Given time, Lizzie will pick herself up too,' he added robustly.

'Of course she will. Time is a great healer,' Laura replied, although she privately wondered if it would be true in the case of Lizzie.

Laura felt a momentary pang of envy for the luxury of Lizzie's life, with servants to do her bidding and Humphrey's wealth and devotion that enabled her to have whatever she wanted. For Laura things had been different. Broken-hearted at seventeen when her fiancé was killed in an accident had been hard enough to bear, but realizing ten years later that her husband was an alcoholic who had spent all their money as a result of his drinking was another matter. Bankruptcy had stripped her of everything. The loss of their lovely house and every single thing in it, even her gold wedding ring, had been enough to break anyone's spirit. For a time she'd been successful with her dressmaking business but the war had reduced her work by more than half. There were moments when she still had to scrape together a few shillings to get something for Caroline's supper.

They'd arrived at the stately house in Cornwall Gardens, and as if by magic the door was opened by the butler as soon as their car drew up outside.

'You go right in, my dear,' Humphrey told Laura, 'and I look forward to seeing you this evening.'

'Thank you for meeting me,' she replied gratefully, thinking him to be one of the nicest men she'd ever met. The trouble was that Lizzie didn't appreciate him.

At that moment the housekeeper, Mrs Hughes, came forward to show Laura to her room. 'Her Ladyship told me to ask if you could see her as soon as you arrived.' She smiled blandly.

Laura was longing for a hot bath and a rest after sitting up all night on a rattling train with a baby crying at intervals, but instead she nodded and said, 'I'll go and see her right away.'

'Would you like me to send up a breakfast tray for you? A cup of tea and some toast perhaps?'

'That would be very nice.'

As soon as Laura saw Lizzie she realized the depths of her grief. Not only were her eyes puffy and red but her whole face was swollen.

'Oh, Laura!' Her voice was husky. 'Thank God you're here.'
Laura hurried over to the bed and kissed her sister on both
cheeks.

'My darling, darling sister,' she said sympathetically. She
cupped Lizzie's face in her hands. 'Are you eating properly,
my love? You look thinner. You mustn't let yourself get sick.
I remember I stopped eating after Rory died. It doesn't change
anything, my darling. It doesn't do any good.'

Lizzie nodded. 'At least you had the rest of your life before
you. I know now my chances of having someone like Justin
in my life again are nil. We were so happy together. Our love
for each other was divine. That's never going to happen again
now that I'm forty.' Tears were streaming down her cheeks and
her voice was husky.

Laura spoke with care. 'I know exactly what you mean,
darling, but you will get over it. One can get over anything
with time. You have a wealth of happy memories and that's
something a lot of people will never experience. Do the girls
know what's happened?'

Lizzie shook her head as she wiped her eyes. 'Humphrey
has told them I've got very bad flu and that they mustn't come
near me in case they catch it. The doctor has given me some
pills but they're not working.' A sob caught in her throat.

'I don't think pills are the answer,' Laura said firmly. 'When
I go back to Scotland why don't you come with me and you
could stay with Mama? I know she'd love to have you and
what you need is walks in the fresh air and to be with family.
What do you think?'

'I don't know what to do.'

'Let's talk it over with Humphrey this evening. You need
to get away from London and have a real break, away from
places that remind you of Justin.'

At that moment there was a knock on the bedroom door.

'Who is it?' Lizzie asked anxiously.

'I have a breakfast tray for Lady Laura, milady,' the maid
replied.

'Oh that's all right. Come in.' Lizzie pulled herself together.
'Haven't you had breakfast, Laura?'

'No.'

'Didn't you come on first class? They usually do a wonderful breakfast.'

Laura waited until the maid had left the room before answering. 'We can't all afford to travel first class, Lizzie. And we certainly can't all afford to wallow in sorrow with our armies of servants to do everything for us, you know.'

Lizzie looked sheepish. 'You think I'm spoilt?'

Laura sipped her tea. 'You are married to a rare gem of a man, who adores you unconditionally, with four beautiful daughters who do you credit, and a beautiful house full of servants to do your bidding – and you wonder if you're spoilt? I don't have to think too long about that one, Lizzie.'

There was a long pause. 'I've hurt Humphrey, haven't I?'

'Massively. But he still loves you and would do anything to make you happy.'

'I'm glad the girls don't know about the affair,' Lizzie said in a small voice. 'They'd think less of me, wouldn't they?'

'It would be very destabilizing, I'm sure. They think of you as such a saint.'

The flickers of a smile hovered around Lizzie's mouth. 'Perhaps I'll have a bath and get dressed.'

'Good idea,' Laura replied. And, although she was suffering from lack of sleep, she added, 'Why don't we go for a brisk walk in Kensington Gardens? It's a lovely day and we could take some bread to feed the birds in the Round Pond.'

An hour later they set off with a paper bag full of crusts, and to Laura's delight, Lizzie was much calmer and stopped crying. She'd never get over Justin's death, but in time she would become resigned to it, along with thousands of other women who had lost their husbands and sons, their fiancés, boyfriends and cousins. This was the bloodiest war the world had ever known and when it finally ended there would be a generation of widows and spinsters.

Six

Rowena led the way into the breakfast room where the parlour maid had laid the table, as well as placing silver entrée dishes on the sideboard offering scrambled eggs, crispy bacon and grilled tomatoes.

'Is Dada coming down for breakfast?' Caroline asked.

'He'll be down in a minute,' her aunt replied.

Walter needed looking after these days and she still resented Laura for wanting a separation when he'd begged her to take him back. 'I could help you both financially at least to start with,' Rowena had told Laura.

'Thank you but I'm perfectly capable of earning enough to keep Caroline and I, and anyway, I don't trust Walter when it comes to drink. He swears he'll never touch another drop but we all know how little his word counts for.'

Laura came down the stairs at that moment and entered the breakfast room saying, 'Good morning,' to her sister-in-law. 'It looks as if it's going to be a lovely day,' she added brightly. What else was there to say? Her relationship with Rowena had always been excruciatingly stilted and polite.

'Yes, but I think it will rain this afternoon,' Rowena replied stiffly, helping herself to scrambled eggs and coffee. Then she sat down at the breakfast table. At that moment Walter appeared, followed by Caroline who had gone to see where he was.

'My darling pet waited on the stairs for me,' he remarked, giving Caroline a tender look. She turned to cast a triumphant smile as if to say to Laura that her dada still adored her.

Laura ignored the look as she calmly helped herself to scrambled eggs and tea.

Walter smiled. 'Come and sit beside me, Caroline.'

There was a glint in her eyes that told everyone that her father loved her and she loved him more than anyone in the whole wide world. Caroline was sure his first wife would have stayed with him, unlike Muzzie, who could be cruel. Neil, her poor stepbrother, had gone to live with his late mother's parents. In her mind's eye, Caroline had painted a picture of happy families, like all her cousins had. If only it were true. Life could have been so different. Now, Dada was deprived of both his son and his daughter. She remembered Rowena speaking in whispered undertones some time ago with undisguised venom, telling everyone how selfish Laura had been.

'Poor Walter,' Rowena had said at the time. 'How could Laura have left him in his hour of need?'

Laura was aware that Caroline was purposely appearing to be more light-hearted than usual, in order to show her mother how happy she was to be with her father. Laura smiled serenely but Caroline continued, 'Dada says he's going to take me shopping this morning,' she announced. 'He's going to buy me a special present.' Her tone was smug.

Laura knew this routine well and it usually ended up costing her several shillings.

'How kind of Dada,' she replied cheerfully. 'I wish I could donate a few pence to your shopping spree but I didn't bring any cash with me. Just our railway tickets.'

Walter flushed uncomfortably. 'You don't have to give any money,' he muttered. 'I've got enough.'

Caroline looked from her mother to her father. 'When I'm the most famous ballerina in the world, I'll be making hundreds of pounds and I'll give you all the money you need, Dada,' she said and she smiled superciliously, as if she had a bad smell under her nose.

Walter's flush deepened. 'No, darling, you must keep your money for yourself.'

But Caroline was determined to make her mother feel bad. 'No, you need it, Dada. Look how worn out your suit is! You need new clothes. Muzzie ought to buy you a new suit. She's making lots of money and she could easily afford it.'

Laura's mouth tightened but she knew this game well; Caroline always played it when she visited her father.

'What have I told you, Caroline?' Laura's tone was sharp.

'It's very vulgar to discuss money in this way. It's something we don't talk about.'

'Your mother's absolutely right,' Walter said firmly, but he was smiling with amusement.

'No, she isn't!' Caroline's voice rose. 'She makes tons of money and she's being mean! She should buy you a new suit.' Then she rose from her chair, flung her napkin down upon the breakfast table and strode out of the room. They heard her stomp up the stairs and finally slam her bedroom door.

Rowena looked pained. 'The trouble is that she sees so little of her father. It seems a pity to have a contretemps when she is staying here.'

'Laura is right though,' Walter confirmed. 'Caroline must be taught how to behave.'

'She's just overexcited at seeing you, Walter,' Rowena insisted.

'Rudeness is rudeness,' he said firmly. 'I think you are a wonderful mother, Laura. I won't talk about taking her shopping again. I don't want to undermine you.'

Laura smiled at him. 'Thank you. She only does it to provoke me, and that isn't fair on either of us.'

'I know, my dear, and I spoil her dreadfully.' He sighed slightly. 'How are her ballet classes going?'

'I have to say, Madame Espinosa is thrilled. She wants Caroline to go professional next year. She's going to introduce her to the right people to see if she can perform in the theatre.'

Walter's face lit up and he clapped his hands. 'That's marvellous! Oh, I always knew she'd be successful.'

'She's already a prima donna,' Rowena observed drily.

Edinburgh, November 1919

Caroline came bounding into the flat as Laura put the finishing touches to a deep purple chiffon ball gown she was making for one of her customers.

'Have you finished my new tutu?' were Caroline's first words to her mother when she returned home from her ballet class.

Laura nodded and pointed to the ballet dress that was on a hanger on the back of the workroom door. It was a white satin bodice with slender shoulder straps, exquisitely shaped, with the layers of white tulle that formed the short tutu around the hips falling delicately in the traditional style. It had taken Laura hours to make, when she should have been working on dresses for her customers, which meant that she'd now have to work late into the night.

Caroline had a one-track mind and everything had to be about her. She never thought about thanking her mother. She was going to be the next Anna Pavlova, wasn't she? One day she'd be the star of *Swan Lake*, rich and famous, with a dressing room full of glorious flowers from admiring fans. Handsome young men would wait for her to emerge from the stage door every night and there'd be a chauffeur-driven car waiting to take her back to her beautiful house.

'What's for supper, Muzzie?' she asked, happy with her daydream.

'Your favourite – stuffed marrow.'

'Again?'

'You know you love it and it's cheap and nourishing. I can get a vegetable marrow for tuppence, and a large onion and a pound of minced beef only cost a few more pence.' Laura had taught herself to cook and the results were so good that Diana had laughingly said if dressmaking failed she could always open a restaurant instead.

Caroline had no interest whatsoever. 'How shall I know when the water's boiling?' she'd asked once when shown how to cook a boiled egg.

'Tomorrow Madame Espinosa is taking me to an audition,' she said excitedly.

Laura looked up from her stitching in delight. 'That's wonderful, darling. What's it for? A new ballet?'

'It's for a solo turn as a butterfly in a new production of *Puss in Boots* at the Theatre Royal.'

'Here in Edinburgh?'

'No, in Timbuktu,' Caroline scoffed. 'Of course it's here. Although I imagine if it's a success it might be put on in London.' Her face was radiant and her dark eyes, so like her father's, sparkled with happiness. At last, her dreams had begun to come true. If she got the part she might have made the first step to performing at Covent Garden Opera House, just like Anna Pavlova.

The next morning she set off with her new tutu and her least-worn ballet shoes in high spirits. Her teacher, who had herself been a prima ballerina some thirty years ago, had told her to wear her ordinary practise leotard, but Caroline was desperate to impress. With her long dark hair coiled into a smooth glossy chignon she bounced off down the street, leaving her mother in a state of nerves. She'd worked day and night for years to allow Caroline to have this chance and she dreaded to think of her daughter's disappointment if she didn't get this small but telling chance to show what she could do.

Laura was certain that once Caroline started climbing the ladder of success she'd be a much happier person. She was sure her daughter's mean and nasty streak was caused by frustration. Once she had the career she craved, Laura was convinced Caroline would feel less of a need to lash out at the people around her.

When the telephone rang shortly before noon the next day Laura hurried to answer it, thinking it was Caroline letting her know how her audition had gone.

'Laura, is that you?' asked the tearful voice of Beattie.

Laura's heart quickened with fear. It was an automatic response after four years of war, when the sound of a ringing phone or the arrival of a telegram could signify the death of a beloved. Georgie's husband, Shane, had lost a leg, and of course Lizzie's lover had been killed.

'Is it Andrew?' she asked without thinking.

There was a stunned silence. 'How did you know?' Beattie sounded angry now.

'I don't know.'

'Do the rest of the family know about the affair too?'

'What?' Laura was confused for a moment. 'I thought you were telephoning me to say that something awful had happened to him.'

Andrew had never been her favourite brother-in-law because he was so boastful. He'd inherited his father's printing works which he now ran, making huge profits, spending lavishly to show just how rich he was. He also boasted that his wife was

'Lady' Beatrice, the daughter of the late Earl of Rothbury. Sometimes he would mournfully add that he should have bought the family seat, Lochlee Castle. The sisters used to joke among themselves that he was 'in trade', and that the happiest day of his life was when, upon his marriage to Beattie, his name became listed in *Burke's Peerage*.

'How do you know he's having an affair?' Laura asked.

'I found a receipt for a fur wrap in his dressing room. It was hidden under his little case of evening studs. What shall I do?' Beattie asked brokenly. 'I nearly died of shock when I found it.'

'Are you sure he hasn't bought a fur for you? It could be a surprise present? Have you got an anniversary coming up?'

'That's what I thought at first, but I've looked everywhere and there's no sign of a fur wrap. Anyway, he gave me a sable coat for my birthday three months ago. I'm so scared, Laura. I never expected anything like this. Do I walk out or am I supposed to turn a blind eye and pretend I've never found this receipt?'

'Are you by any chance pregnant again? You know how he lavishes expensive presents on you when there's another baby on the way,' Laura asked thoughtfully, remembering the diamond and emerald necklace when their first child had been born.

There was a long pause before Beattie replied. 'No. I'm not pregnant. I can't be because we haven't been . . . you know. He's been sleeping in his dressing room.' Her voice broke and she struggled to go on. 'He says he has to get up early, and, and . . . he doesn't want to disturb me.' She choked on her tears. 'At first I thought he was being con-con-considerate. And now . . .'

Laura's heart sank. 'Is there a date on this receipt?'

'Yes. March the twelfth. Eight months ago.'

'How long have you been sleeping apart?' Laura asked, dreading the answer.

Again, a long pause before Beattie answered. 'Just after Christmas. He's expanding the business and he warned me I'd see less of him for a few months. That's true. He leaves at dawn and doesn't get home until late.'

Laura recognized the desperation in her sister's voice. It was obvious that Beattie was trying to persuade herself that everything was all right in her marriage.

'Do you think I can win him back?' Beattie asked. 'What are the children going to say?'

Henry had just turned fifteen and the two youngest, Kathleen and Camilla, were eight and seven years old. Beattie was aware that if she and Andrew parted it would shatter them. If only for the children's sake she must preserve her marriage, no matter that Andrew was breaking her heart. Her voice was steady now. 'I've got to get through this as best as I can, haven't I? I must make my marriage work somehow.'

'That's right,' Laura agreed. 'If I was in your shoes I'd try to forget you ever found that wretched receipt and I'd organize several big and rather grand dinner parties. I'd make sure all the guests were titled; you know how Andrew would adore that. You must butter him up by telling him how popular he is and how they'll invite him to go shooting with them. He'll think he's gone to heaven and that you're an angel.'

'You mean that I should make his home life so exciting and diverting that he'll want to stay with me?'

Laura could detect the reluctance in her voice, but she spoke firmly. 'Be honest, Beattie. I think you married him for his money and he married you because you've got a title.'

There was a long pause on the other end of the line and Laura feared for a moment that she'd spoken too freely. But then Beattie spoke resignedly, 'It's true. I suppose you're right. But my God, Laura, that's not what's making me stay. It's my babies. I won't let them be hurt by their father's folly.'

Laura remained silent. She knew how difficult Caroline had become, simply because Laura refused to live with Walter because he was a bankrupt alcoholic. 'You're right,' she told her sister. 'You can't let it affect the children's lives. Let me know how you get on, Beattie.'

'Oh, I will. And thank you for the advice, Laura. You don't know what it means.'

Laura was still thinking about Beattie when Caroline came hurtling in to the workroom, her face radiant with happiness. She shouted, 'I've got it! I got the part of the butterfly and we start rehearsing on Monday!'

Laura sprang to her feet and flung her arms around her daughter. All their hopes and dreams were becoming reality. All the years of hard slog as a dressmaker and Caroline's unstinting ballet practise were bearing fruit and how wonderfully rewarding it was now.

'Oh, darling, I'm so proud of you. Why don't you telephone Dada and tell him the good news? He'll be so proud of you too.'

While Caroline regaled her father with details of her achievement, Laura sat gazing into space, trying to take it all in. Caroline's dedication to ballet was to be admired and Madame Espinosa had always recognized Caroline's talent. This could be her big chance to show everyone just how brilliant a dancer she was.

'Dada says he'll come to my opening night,' Caroline said jubilantly. 'He and Aunt Rowena are going to book tickets tomorrow. You'd better get some too. It's going to be a big pantomime and we might even go on tour,' she added importantly.

Laura smiled at the 'we'. It was obvious that Caroline was going to thrive on being a part of a group with one clear ambition: to perform on stage. She was going to love the camaraderie, the closeness that Laura had found with all her sisters. Caroline had missed out on that by being an only child. This was her first step into the big wide world and Laura couldn't suppress a pang of sorrow because she knew she'd be left behind. That was the order of things and that was why her mother had – somewhat selfishly – kept her youngest daughter, Catriona, close to her side, unmarried, her constant companion.

Laura beamed as Caroline hung up her tutu, hiding her moment of sadness as she asked, 'What sort of costume will you wear as a butterfly?'

Caroline shrugged. 'I don't know. The wardrobe mistress said she'd arrange all that.'

'Won't the opening night be exciting? I'll get Aunt Di and Uncle Robert to come and I think Granny and Aunt Catriona would love to see your debut, too.'

Caroline rolled her dark eyes. 'Oh, for heaven's sake! It will look dreadful if the stalls are filled with the family up from the country to see me dance! I'm a professional ballerina now. I'm more interested in what the theatre critics think of my performance.' She picked up her handbag. 'I've got to go. I'm meeting a friend for supper.' A moment later she was gone and Laura felt the first link in the chain between them break. Her little girl was almost a grown woman now.

Seven

Edinburgh, November 1919

'Who, pray, is Miss Cooper?' Laura asked as she sat down by the telephone in her workroom.

'Andrew's secretary.' Beattie's voice sounded flat, as though she'd come to terms with her marital problems. 'She's the woman he's been having an affair with for the past year.'

'How do you know it's her?'

'He finally confessed and he's told me everything. He's madly in love with her.'

'Oh my God! Are you all right, darling? You sound terribly calm. If he's confessed she was his mistress does that mean you've patched things up? Oh, I do hope so, Beattie. The close proximity of working together for long hours was probably the cause of his emotional aberration. Has she gone now?'

'If you mean has she given up her job and moved on the answer is no. In due course she'll be the next Mrs Drinkwater. Why should she move on?' Beattie's voice was expressionless.

'What do you mean?' Laura felt stunned. The implications of what Beattie was saying were too dreadful. 'You surely can't be getting a divorce? No one in the family has ever been divorced. What about the children, Beattie? Why are you letting him get away with all this? Think of the stigma surrounding divorce! Think how it will affect and follow the children!' Laura's face and neck were flushed and her voice was raised. She desperately wanted Beattie to avoid such drastic action. 'Why don't you just live separately like Walter and I? There is no scandal attached to a separation and you can remain civil to each other and avoid notoriety. There's no need for lawyers to get involved, and it's much nicer for the children.'

'I know, Laura. You don't think I know all this? It's nothing to do with me. It's Andrew. He's insisting on a divorce because he wants to marry Miss Cooper as quickly as possible because . . . Well, I might as well tell you – everyone will know soon enough. She's expecting a baby.'

'What?' Laura hands were shaking and she'd risen to her feet with anger. 'You can't let him get away with this. He's got to be brought to his senses.' Beattie had always been the sweet and shy one in the family, and this wretched man was taking advantage of her good nature. Andrew's actions were utterly unforgivable. 'Listen, Beattie, have you talked to Lizzie and Di? Humphrey and Robert should talk to Andrew and tell him he simply can't behave like this.'

Beattie sounded tired and weary. 'I honestly don't think it would do any good. The way things stand I don't have much say in the matter. If I don't agree to a divorce he won't give me a penny. He's already said as much. The children and I will be paupers. As it stands I can keep this house and he'll give me enough to live on as I do now and he will pay for everything.'

'Oh my God, you must get a good lawyer. There's no way you can fight this . . . this madness on your own. The man's a bully and you're letting him get away with it. The law won't allow him to leave you penniless if you don't comply with his demands. What sort of a hold has he got over you?'

'Would you want to stay with a man who calls you dull and boring? Who tells me my whole family is snobbish and looks down on him? He's deeply disappointed I didn't have even one son who could take over his business one day. I've said we could try for another baby but he replied I'd probably have "another bloody girl". I hate him, Laura. I want a quiet divorce so that I can live my life in comfort with my children.'

'Oh, Beattie, I'm so sorry,' Laura said. 'You deserve someone who will really look after you. Let me know if there is anything I can do.'

'Thank you, Laura. Gosh, who would have thought it? Who would have thought that I would be the first member of the family to be divorced?' The line went dead as she hung up.

Cranley Court, November 1919

Lady Rothbury and Catriona were staying with Diana when the news broke. Lizzie and Humphrey had secured a good lawyer for Beattie, who was still protesting that Andrew's proposed financial offer was more than acceptable.

'Has the girl gone out of her mind?' Her mother was filled with a mixture of fury and pity. 'We mustn't allow Beattie to get a divorce. We've never had the disgrace of a divorce in the family, and we never will. Not on my watch.'

'Unfortunately, these days it seems to be more and more common,' Robert pointed out sadly.

'Maybe it has for common people but not families like ours,' the countess retorted sharply. 'An aristocratic man might have a mistress, but it will be a discreet affair and the wife will accept it to avoid a scandal. Look at Queen Alexandra. Bertie is in every woman's bed except his wife's now they have a family. One of her ladies-in-waiting told me that the Queen won't go to bed herself until the King returns home to the palace.'

'The poor Queen,' Diana said sadly. 'She's so beautiful, too. Do you really want Beattie to have all that heartbreak and humiliation, Mama?'

'No, but they could separate like Laura and Walter. Then lawyers wouldn't have to be involved and the whole matter could be handled quietly and tastefully. If there's a divorce there will be no way of keeping it out of the papers. She can forget about being invited to Buckingham Palace, or being admitted to the Royal Enclosure at Ascot. You don't seem to realize what a calamity it would be.'

'I'm more concerned with Beattie's happiness than her social standing,' Diana exclaimed stubbornly. 'Who cares about that sort of thing nowadays?'

'Diana, think of how it will affect her children. Why should they pay the price of their parents' folly? This situation needs to be handled with care and diplomacy.'

There was silence in the room. Lady Rothbury had spoken and Diana and Catriona looked subdued, while Robert decided it was the right moment to leave the discussion.

'I've got letters to write, dearest,' he said, affectionately patting his wife on the shoulder. 'I'll see you all later.'

'What does Laura think about all this?' Catriona asked when he'd left the room.

'Laura said she thinks Beattie should put up a fight,' Diana replied. 'The point is that this woman is expecting a baby. She may be the one who is pressing him to get a divorce and marry her because she's after his money. He is enormously wealthy, you know.'

Lady Rothbury leaned forward and spoke urgently. 'Then why doesn't someone suggest to Andrew that he buys this woman a house and give her some money and then leave her to get on with it? My God, if every man married his mistress because he'd got her pregnant the divorce rate would increase by half!'

'Mama, that's a brilliant idea. Poor Beattie. She must be going through hell. My advice to her would be to sit tight for the sake of the children. And I don't think she should tell anyone outside the family,' Diana murmured.

'Absolutely right,' her mother agreed. 'If I were in Beattie's shoes I'd start by giving a few really grand dinner parties so Andrew has something to look forward to in his own home. She should invite people who would be useful to him in business – people this girl couldn't dream of knowing. Men are essentially cowards. They hate confrontation and they're like naughty children. They know what they're doing is wrong, but if the wife ignores the affair it loses its excitement. Beattie should ignore the fact he has a mistress. She should go out and buy herself some beautiful clothes. She should learn to play bridge. She should organize amusing things for them to do together. With a man like Andrew things have got to be made exciting. He was never the sort of man who would come home in the evening and sit by the fire reading the newspapers.' Her own husband, the father of her eleven children, had confessed on his deathbed he'd kept a mistress who had given birth to a son. The family only became aware of the child's existence when, as a grown man, he'd returned to claim his inheritance. The Earl of Rothbury refused to acknowledge him because he was a bastard, telling him that if he used the Rothbury coat of arms he would make sure that it would have the Baton Sinister across it to mark his illegitimacy. The man put a curse on the whole family and for the next few years they were followed by tragedy. Her husband and both her sons had died and one of her daughters, Eleanor, was killed in a mysterious accident.

Lady Rothbury closed her eyes for a minute as the terrible memories came back as vividly as when they had happened. The curse of the Rowan tree had only ceased when the tree was uprooted and burnt one night by a stranger.

Without heirs the noble title of the Earl of Rothbury was now extinct and Lochlee Castle was sold because three lots of death duties had ruined them financially.

Meanwhile, Diana was sure that if Andrew had married someone fiery like Laura he wouldn't have been tempted to have an affair in the first place. Before Walter had become bankrupt, and permanently ruined his health with drink, Laura had been a sparkling hostess, filling their house with interesting and lively people. Her Christmas parties had been full of surprises, like the year Father Christmas entered the house on a donkey with presents for everyone. Then, every November the fifth, she'd invite all their friends to a firework display in their big garden while her staff offered everyone a warming glass of spiced mulled wine.

Poor Beattie didn't have that *joie de vivre*. None of them did. Of the nine daughters Laura was the strongest, the wittiest and the most charismatic, in spite of all the hard times she'd been through.

Lady Rothbury rose slowly to her feet. 'Could you help me up the stairs, Catriona? And then if you could fetch me a glass of water and my pills I'll have a little rest.'

Catriona smiled, barely listening because her mother's requests were predictable and the same every day.

Edinburgh, December 1919

Caroline had no idea it would be such hard work. Ballet classes were pleasurable, very precise and exacting but enormously gratifying when Madame Espinosa exclaimed 'Bravo!' when Caroline completed a series of pirouettes, her head whipping around with each turn at exactly the correct angle.

Rehearsing for a stage show where the choreographer changed his mind every few minutes was another matter. This was the moment she'd always dreamed of, and it was a shock to be shouted at, criticized and sometimes sworn at. By the end of each day she was exhausted and ready to weep with frustration. She was the only ballerina in the show. All the other dancers were showgirls who performed together as a group, and she couldn't help but feel left out when they had a welcome break and sat around chatting to each other. Instead of trying to join them she appeared aloof and snobbish so they made no attempt to be friendly.

'I'm a ballerina, not a showgirl,' she said to Laura one evening when she returned from rehearsals. 'I'm a solo artist. I've been picked to give this show a bit of class.'

Laura's heart sank. She knew nothing about the theatre and had never even met an actor, but gut instinct told her that the way to get on and be liked in any place was to be friendly and charming.

'Why don't you take a tin of biscuits or a cake with you tomorrow? Share it with the other dancers and . . .'

Caroline jumped to her feet and swore angrily. 'Damn it! I'm not going to make them my friends. They're all so common.'

Laura spoke firmly. 'Please do not swear under my roof. It seems to me they don't want to be friends with you because you're a snob. You do not refer to people as "common". From where do you get this attitude? Not me or your father. I'm not surprised they don't like you if you appear to look down on them. I read a quote in a newspaper from a famous actress, who said, "You're only as good as your last performance." Remember that, my girl, if you want to get on.'

'Oh, I hate you . . .!' Caroline burst out in a tearful rage. Then she marched to the bedroom and slammed the door.

Laura sat deep in thought. It was true that this was only a pantomime and perhaps Madame Espinosa had made a mistake in sending her to the audition? Surely after all the years of training Caroline should be trying to get into a ballet company? In the meantime, Laura decided to keep her thoughts to herself, but a plan was forming in her mind. It would mean enormous sacrifices and changes in their lives, and she didn't know how she was going to finance it, but something had to be done, or she feared that Caroline would never get anywhere.

The Theatre Royal, Edinburgh 1919

There was a palpable throb of excitement in the stalls and dress circle as the audience waited for the red velvet curtain to rise on the first night of *Puss in Boots*.

Laura had invited her mother, Catriona, Diana and Georgie, as well as their husbands and children, to come and see Caroline's first public performance.

Walter and Rowena had also invited some of their friends, so it was a merry group that were seated in the two front rows of the dress circle.

The theatre was packed and the excitement reached fever point when the musicians entered the orchestra pit. Some children started clapping when the violinists began to tune their instruments.

Walter, who was sitting beside Laura, nudged her with his elbow. 'I'm as nervous as hell. Suppose she forgets her steps?' he muttered. 'What about you? Aren't you nervous too?'

'I think I'm past being nervous. If we can get through tonight then we can get through anything,' Laura said grimly. 'I'll be thankful when it's over.'

Walter chuckled and patted her hand. 'That's my Laura! Able to cope with anything. You've done a wonderful job bringing her up, and it can't have been easy.'

'We've had our moments,' she replied drily.

At that moment the conductor raised his baton and the orchestra struck up a jolly overture.

'Oh, God! Here we go,' Walter groaned under his breath.

It was a typical pantomime to begin with and Laura allowed herself to relax and even laugh at the corny jokes. She began to wonder when Caroline would make her debut. The show seemed to drag on for ages, and she wondered if they'd cut out Caroline's performance altogether. Anxiety made her blood run cold. Had Caroline had a fall? Broken her ankle perhaps? At that moment the stage went dark except for a beam of light on a piece of scenery that resembled a giant leaf. The music changed too, becoming gentle and poignant . . . Laura caught her breath. A butterfly was slowly unfolding its wings as if waking from a deep sleep. The wings flapped a few times and then the butterfly flew off the leaf and hovered as if in mid-air. It whirled and seemed to flutter, dipping and swooping gracefully. The stage was filled with bright lights and the butterfly seemed to revel in the sunshine. Then a clap of thunder startled the audience and the stage went dark. Flashes of lightning and more thunder saw the butterfly struggling to survive the summer storm. The music soared dramatically and the butterfly seemed to fall to the ground and lie there, helpless. A minute later the storm passed and the brave little butterfly fluttered and then flew back to the safety of the giant leaf as the sun shone once more.

The stage blacked out and the applause was deafening. People in the stalls were standing and shouting 'Bravo!' and 'Encore!' and the clapping continued for several minutes.

Laura looked at Walter and his cheeks were wet with tears. He reached for her hand. 'To think that was our little girl,' he murmured with awe.

Laura was doing her best to control her own emotions so she nodded, aware that the rest of the family were looking at her. She knew now that Caroline deserved to be in a proper ballet company. No matter what it meant, as soon as this pantomime closed she would announce her plans, though God only knew how she was going to finance them.

Dalkeith House, a week later

'What are you doing, Walter?' Rowena asked sharply. 'Those are my best scissors.'

He beamed and held up a cutting from *The Scotsman*. 'Caroline has got the most marvellous reviews! All the newspapers are raving about her.' He shuffled through a pile of newspapers with boyish excitement. 'I bought a scrapbook when I was out so that I could keep them all safe.'

Rowena surprised herself as her eyes began to sting with emotion. At that moment she felt an acute pang of pity for the brother who had lost his wife and children and beautiful home because of his alcoholism. His son, Neil, had been a troubled child after his mother had died, and he'd resented Laura and kept setting fire to the house. For the past few years his mother's parents had looked after him. Laura had left Walter after he'd gone bankrupt and he only saw Caroline, whom he adored, occasionally. Unable to work any more, he'd have ended up in the poorhouse if she hadn't taken pity on him and said he could live with her.

'Listen to this,' Walter was saying as he picked up a cutting. 'It says, "Caroline Harvey delighted the audience with her debut as a ballerina." This other one says: "A true star was born on the first night of *Puss in Boots* when Caroline Harvey received a standing ovation for her exquisite precision and gracefulness. Her solo performance of a butterfly caught in a storm thrilled the audience . . . She moves with poetic grace." Isn't that absolutely splendid?'

'Very good,' Rowena agreed. But then added gently: 'I wonder how she'd do if she ever got the chance to perform at Covent Garden in London? We're in the provinces here and the local reviewers are very easily pleased.'

Walter looked deeply offended. 'You never did like ballet, did you? Or opera. Madame Espinosa wouldn't have trained Caroline if she thought she was not going to make it.'

Rowena shrugged. 'Laura paid her well. In fact, most of what she earned as a dressmaker went to pay Madame Espinosa. I have always thought it was a mistake to encourage Caroline to go on the stage. It's the most precarious way of making a living. She ought to have been trained for a proper job in case she doesn't marry well.'

Walter looked at her with the expression of a wounded dog. 'For goodness' sake, she's just a young girl! Give her a chance! No doubt she'll marry whether she's a dancer or not. Laura and I think she's got a brilliant future either way.'

'She's no longer a child, Walter. I was almost a bride at her age,' Rowena replied tartly. 'I don't think it's right to let a young woman presume she's one of the Seven Wonders of the World. It's a real burden for her to have to live up to all this expectation. She'll is terribly disappointed if she finds herself in pantomimes year after year.'

Walter placed the cuttings carefully between the pages of the scrapbook without saying a word, then marched out of the room, slamming the door behind him.

The Theatre Royal, two months later

Groaning in pain, Caroline sank on to the bed in her dressing room and, bending down, untied the ribbons around her ankles. Then, slowly and carefully, she withdrew first one foot and then the other out of her white satin pointe shoes.

'Oh . . .' she whimpered. 'Look at my poor feet!'

Laura, who was sitting in the corner, looked sympathetic. 'Take off your tights and I'll wash them.'

'Look at all the blood!' Caroline gave a self-pitying little sob. 'My toes are in agony. I need to bathe them in warm water . . . I need iodine . . .' She leaned back, pulling the wreath of artificial flowers from her head.

There was a tap on the door and a stagehand opened it without waiting and, rushing in, thrust a bouquet of pink carnations in her direction. 'It says Mademoiselle Zeni on the label,' he scoffed. 'If you're French then I'm the King of England.' He shot off again, chuckling to himself, 'Who the hell does she think she is, the snobbish cow?'

Laura raised her eyebrows and spoke. 'I told you it was a mistake to give yourself a stage name. And a foreign one at that!'

'But Madame Espinosa said I'd get much further with a French name and she should know.' Dabbing her toes with warm water, Caroline said sulkily, 'You don't know what you're talking about! This is my career and I'll do what I want.'

Her mother replied spiritedly, 'You seem to have forgotten I had to earn the money to pay for all your ballet classes for over ten years. For goodness' sake, I chaperone you home every night when you finish here. I know what people are saying about you. You've let a few good reviews go to your head. You're not Anna Pavlova yet.'

'People are just jealous of me,' Caroline said shrilly.

At that moment there was another tap on the door. 'It'll be more flowers,' she jeered boastingly.

Instead an elderly gentleman wearing a military uniform entered the room. 'Dada!' she shrieked, jumping to her feet, her painful toes forgotten. She reached up and flung her arms around his neck.

'That was the best performance you've given yet, my darling,' he declared as he gave her a beaming smile. 'You were magnificent. And now look your poor toes, my little sweetheart.'

Watching them, Laura felt a pang of jealousy at their devotion to each other.

'Dada!' Caroline repeated, her face alight with joy at his presence. 'Muzzie is objecting to my stage name but you think it will help my career, don't you?'

Walter smiled at Laura. 'I think your mother is right. You are already known as Caroline Harvey, so why change it? I agree that Leighton-Harvey would be a mouthful. To me Mademoiselle Zeni smacks of a Cabaret dancer in a Paris nightclub,' he added firmly. 'I agree with your mother. To change your name would be mad, not to mention dishonest. We don't have a drop of French blood in our veins.'

Caroline stepped back and flung herself on to her chair. 'Neither of you know anything about the theatre,' she snapped. 'I've got to get an agent . . .'

Laura looked up in surprise. 'I thought Madame Espinosa was advising you.'

'She's my teacher and mentor. What I need, as soon as this show closes, is a professional agent who will promote me and get me work.'

Laura turned pale. 'How much will that cost?'

Caroline tossed her head and cast her eyes up. 'For goodness' sake, all you think about is money. You don't pay an agent anything. They deduct a percentage of what I get paid. You see?'

'There's no need to be rude to your mother.' Walter looked shaken by her hostility. Why was Caroline behaving like this when she had the world at her feet? 'I expect you're very tired,' he said quietly. 'I'll slip away now so you can go home and get some sleep.' As he turned to leave Laura went up to him and laid her hand on his shoulder. He'd looked so disappointed at Caroline's rudeness that she felt sorry for him.

'She's absolutely exhausted, but thank you for coming to tonight's performance.'

He smiled. 'I had hoped to take you both out for a bite to eat . . . but maybe another time would be better.'

She nodded, afraid to speak, as a wave of pity for the man she'd once been in love with overwhelmed her.

Eight

London, 1920

Beattie looked drained of energy as she lay back on the sofa in her large and beautiful drawing room in their Belgravia mansion. When Andrew had married her he'd insisted that when Lochlee castle was sold he would look after as many of the Fairbairn family portraits as possible, many of which had been painted by renowned artists. At the time, Lady Rothbury was grateful because she didn't have the space for them at the manse, but Laura had scoffed and declared her brother-in-law only wanted them because: 'He thinks it will give him a touch of class. Why,' she added, 'don't you give him some of the crested silver and be done with it?'

As Beattie gazed around the room, she knew Laura had been right. 'I was bought, wasn't I?' Beattie observed in a quiet voice.

'How do you mean?' Lizzie asked. They'd had lunch in the opulent dining room, waited on by Briggs, the butler, so the conversation had to be impersonal and general in front of the staff. Now on their own, they could talk freely.

'Andrew married me for my background and title and I was stupid enough to think he loved me.'

'If that had been the case, Beattie, he wouldn't be leaving you now. I think he did love you but in the end found he couldn't keep up with you. In spite of his money I think he's rather insecure. Do you remember when we all went to Scotland to stay with Di how he bragged about having first-class tickets for the train, and then three cars to meet you all at the station? Robert could hardly keep a straight face.'

'That's typical of Andrew. I'm sure things between us might have been better if I'd had another son. He was furious when our third baby turned out to be another girl. You'd have thought I'd done it on purpose to spite him!'

'It would serve him right if this woman has twin girls,' Laura said angrily. 'Do the children know what's happening? They must have realized something's up.'

Beattie shook her head. 'Andrew doesn't want a scandal any more than I do, so he's still living here, but of course he sleeps in his dressing room.'

'What about the servants? Are you sure they're not going to gossip?'

'They'd be deaf and blind if they didn't know we are splitting up, but Andrew pays them over the odds so I think they want to keep their jobs.'

'If you get on the right side of the staff and pay them well they're very loyal. They must have guessed when I was having an affair, and when Justin was killed they were extraordinarily tactful. Nobody asked for a moment why I might be spending weeks on end in bed, sending my meals downstairs untouched.'

'And Humphrey? How was he?' Beattie enquired. 'I'm now in the position he was in seven years ago.'

Lizzie smiled. 'He pretended nothing was amiss. He slept in his dressing room for months, saying he had to get up at dawn because of work at the War Office. It was as if Justin had never existed. It was months before we got back to normal – whatever normal is.'

'Poor you. That was the saddest situation and you've been very brave. I wish I were like you and Laura. You're so strong and resilient.'

'So are you, dearest. Facing adversity is what makes you strong and you're being very brave.'

To her surprise, Andrew didn't come back that night. Beattie lay awake, imagining him staying with Beryl Cooper, making love and planning their future together with their new baby. In her head she painted a picture of deep affection and harmony as they planned their life together. She recalled how it had been when Kathleen was born. Andrew had been very tender and loving, telling her again and again how proud he was of her. The memory brought tears to her eyes and she wished with all her heart their marriage had lasted. What had gone so wrong? Why had he fallen in love with his secretary? In the early hours she fell into a fitful sleep and then, suddenly, a door slamming shut awakened her. There was someone in Andrew's dressing room and they were opening and shutting drawers noisily.

'Is that you, Andrew?' she shouted in alarm. There was a sudden dead silence.

Beattie jumped out of bed and flung open the door. Andrew had his back to her and he was leaning against a chest of drawers, his head bowed. He was wearing one of his white shirts and as he raised his hands to cover his face Beattie saw his cuffs were covered with blood.

'Andrew? What's happened?' Her voice was shrill with terror. 'Have you been in an accident?'

He shook his head slowly and she realized he was crying. Deep sobs were being wrenched from his chest and he wouldn't look at her.

'Has someone attacked you?' she persisted, a part of her fearful that he'd got into trouble and another part of her wanting to comfort him.

'She started haemorrhaging,' he blurted out. 'The baby wasn't due for another three months and she started bleeding. I called an ambulance but there was nothing I could do to save him.' He broke down completely and she couldn't make out what he was saying but the one word that lingered in the air was 'him'. So Beryl Cooper had lost the treasured second son that Andrew so wanted. Filled with a rush of pity, she said, 'I'm so sorry, Andrew. To lose a child is always tragic.'

'There won't be another one either,' he replied, looking up at her. 'Beryl died too. They did everything they could but it was no good. They couldn't save her.' His face was ravaged by grief and a painful stab of jealousy shot through her. Would he have felt grief like this if she'd died in childbirth? She imagined not. Her mother would say that this tragedy was God's punishment for the way he had treated his wife.

Beattie, practical as always, said in a calm voice, 'Take off that shirt, Andrew. I'll soak it in cold water to remove the stains. There's no point in letting the servants know what has happened.'

Like an obedient child, he took it off and she carried it to the adjoining bathroom where she held the cuffs under running water. Her head was in a whirl and she'd no idea what the future held now. At last, the stains were gone and she draped the shirt over the radiator. Tomorrow she'd tell the chambermaid that her husband had spilled red wine down his front. On her way back to her own room she looked into Andrew's dressing room. He was lying on his side and he was fast asleep.

Beattie no longer knew how she felt towards him. Affection? Hope that they might now grow closer again? Or was it just pity?

The Manse, 1920

Catriona's hands trembled as she reached for the telephone that stood on a table in the hall of her mother's house. Having to make this call was something she'd always known was inevitable but had hoped wouldn't happen for several years.

'Is that you, Laura?' she asked when she got through.

'Yes. Is that you, Catriona? How are you?'

'I'm all right but I'm afraid that Mama is ill. Very ill. I think you should come. The doctor has been twice and he says her heart is the problem,' she added shakily.

There was a moment's silence before Laura spoke. 'Has she had a heart attack?'

'Not exactly. Last night she had what I thought was an asthma attack. She seemed to have difficulty in breathing and she could hardly speak, so I called the doctor right away. He said her heart wasn't pumping properly. Cardio asthma, I think he called it. It's heart failure in other words because she's old. I'm so frightened, Laura. Can you come? I don't think I can do this on my own.'

'Of course I'll come, darling, and I'll let the others know. Aren't Alice and Flora with you? They only live a few minutes away.'

There was a painful pause. 'We don't really get on that well,' Catriona explained haltingly. 'They call me Mama's pet and they think I'm wasting my life by staying at home with her. Alice said she'd come over this evening and Flora asked me to keep her informed on the telephone.'

'Thank God you are at home with Mama. She might have died if you hadn't been there to call the doctor. Darling, don't let the others bully you. Your life is your own and you can do what you like with it. I'll arrange for a friend to keep an eye on Caroline and I'll be with you by this afternoon.'

'Oh, Laura, thank you. You've no idea how grateful I am. The doctor said Mama must have complete rest to give her heart time to recover but you know what she's like. I think she walked the dogs too far yesterday.' Catriona sank into a nearby chair, weak with relief. Only Laura understood her devotion to their mother. She also liked living in the manse, although it was a dismal house, nothing like Lochlee Castle.

Upstairs in the four-poster bed with its heavy pink brocade drapes, Margaret Rothbury lay, pale-faced and weak, propped up by snowy white pillows. The doctor had insisted it was better for her heart to stay upright rather than lie down. She loved this bed, and had insisted on taking it with her when they'd left the castle. In this very bed she had lost her virginity after her marriage to William, the 6th Earl of Rothbury, and over the years she'd given birth to nine daughters and two sons lying in this exact spot. The first heir, Freddie, had brought nothing but disgrace to the family, eventually dying in a Parisian brothel after years of debauchery. Then Henry, the next heir in line, who was adored by everyone, was killed in the Boer War.

As she languished in the bed, her mind drifted back to the past, remembering the tragedies that had befallen the family. Little Eleanor's death in an extraordinary accident as she tried to get rid of the curse planted on the Fairbairn family was perhaps the worst. She could never forgive the jealous, illegitimate son of her husband who had cursed the entire family when told he could never inherit the family title.

Wife, mother and grandmother; she'd fulfilled her role from the beginning with a strong sense of forbearance. Even when she found she'd married a man who loved his horses and dogs more than his wife and children. Even when her son killed the stable lad in suspicious circumstances. She knew she had done her duty, and for the first time she felt ready to meet her Maker, unafraid and with no regrets. There was only one thing she fretted about now. Months ago she'd made a new will which had rather shocked her lawyer. He'd asked her why she'd changed it so dramatically. After explaining her reasons, she'd had the feeling that he understood her point of view. Nevertheless, there were certainly still moments when she wondered if she'd made the right decision.

Laura arrived later in the afternoon to be greeted by Catriona.

'I don't want Mama to think everyone has come to say goodbye to her,' she said in a low voice. 'Her heart is very weak but it doesn't mean she's going to die in the next few hours, so tell her you are staying for a few days' rest or you're on a trip buying some fabrics for clients.'

Laura looked doubtful. 'Mama is not easily fooled,' she pointed out. 'Anyhow, there's no need to be so pessimistic. She might get over this and, with rest, live for another few years.'

Catriona's face lit up with hope. 'Do you really think so?'

'Let's talk to the doctor and see what he thinks. When is he coming back?'

'At seven o'clock this evening.'

Laura took off her hat. 'Let's go up and see Mama now. She's always been a very strong person and maybe this is just a sign she ought to take things more easily. She is seventy-six.'

Their mother was dozing when they tiptoed into her room but she sensed their presence and opened her eyes. 'What are you doing here, Laura?' she asked and Laura was shocked by the frailty in her voice. Margaret Rothbury normally had a powerful voice that often reached formidable volumes. Now she sounded like a very weak old lady, which, Laura suddenly realized, she in fact was.

'I decided to take a few days off from work so I've come to see you,' Laura replied. 'How are you feeling, Mama? Catriona tells me you haven't been very well,' she added, keeping her own voice light and breezy.

'You mean you've come all this way to see me before I die,' Lady Rothbury said with a faint touch of her usual acerbity. 'There's no point in denying it and I'm very glad to see you.'

'Doctor Harvey says you just need a few days' rest,' Catriona said firmly.

Her mother smiled wanly. 'There's no point in denying the truth, darling. Your father came to see me last night and he wanted me to go home with him.'

Catriona and Laura exchanged knowing looks. It wasn't the first time Lady Rothbury had seen ghosts and it was proof to her that there was life after death. After Eleanor was killed she had sworn for weeks that she'd seen her ghost in the garden near the Rowan tree.

'What did Papa say?' Laura asked.

'He said it was time that I went with him.'

Catriona asked, 'What did you reply, Mama?'

'I told him I wasn't ready. But now, I think I am.'

London, 1920

Beattie knocked on the dressing-room door at eight o'clock the next morning. She was loath to wake up Andrew but he had to be told what had happened.

'Andrew? Are you awake? I've had an urgent telephone call from Laura. My mother had another sort of heart attack in the night and she is seriously ill. I've got to leave to be with her. Lizzie and Humphrey are picking me up and we're catching a train.'

Andrew appeared in the doorway, his face wrecked by grief and exhaustion, but he rallied, looking at her sympathetically. 'Do you want me to come with you? I can be ready in just a jiffy.'

She looked surprised. 'No, you can't possibly come,' she exclaimed in a practical voice. 'You've got problems of your own.' There was a courteous calm between them, as if the past was the past. He'd lost the woman he'd loved and his longed-for baby boy, and she was about to lose her beloved mother.

'I'm sorry. So very sorry,' he blurted out. 'Is there anything I can do?'

'Can you keep an eye on the children? I've told Nanny why I'm rushing off but the girls don't know about their grandmother. I'll . . .' Her voice broke. 'I'll tell them when I return.'

Andrew ran his hand through his tousled hair in a gesture of despair. 'Poor Beattie. Keep in touch, won't you?'

She averted her face and wondered which of them was suffering the most. ''Bye,' she said in a muffled voice as she turned to go downstairs. Her lady's maid had done her packing, quickly collecting together some black dresses, stockings, hats and gloves. Lizzie and Humphrey would be arriving in their chauffeur-driven Rolls-Royce in a few minutes and she was profoundly thankful not to have to travel all the way to Scotland alone. They would get there in time to tell Mama how much they'd always loved her.

As they drove to the station, Lizzie turned to Beattie and said, 'Does Andrew even know you're going away? Or is he too busy looking after the pregnant Miss Cooper?'

Beattie's face betrayed no emotion. Through clenched jaws, she replied, 'Miss Cooper and her baby son died yesterday evening. I don't wish to talk about it.'

Lizzie and Humphrey shared a shocked look. Then, pulling herself together, Lizzie declared briskly, 'Right! Then we won't.'

The Manse, the next evening

Extra chairs had been brought into Lady Rothbury's bedroom as the eight sisters drifted in and out of the room, talking quietly while their mother slept, then saying a few comforting words to her when she awoke. The local doctor called morning and evening, pronouncing her to be a basically strong woman with a will of iron but a heart which could no longer support her.

'Hopefully she'll slip away in her sleep,' he told the family, 'and it could be at any time.'

Two nurses worked in shifts to give her blanket baths and sips of beef tea and to make sure she was comfortable. While all the sisters hovered around, the husbands went for walks with Catriona's spaniels or they sat in the study, talking and putting the world to rights. Everyone met for lunch while one of the nurses sat beside Lady Rothbury's bed having promised to alert them if there was any change in Her Ladyship's condition. An atmosphere of resignation and calm pervaded the

house as each sister began to accept that one day everyone has
to die.

'Did you know that Andrew's mistress has died?' Lizzie
whispered to Diana when they were alone.

'No! When did this happen?'

'Very recently. Don't mention it, though. Beattie doesn't
want to talk about it. She was looking very shaken when we
picked her up in the car. The baby apparently died also.'

Diana looked shocked. 'How terrible,' she said gravely. Then,
after a long pause, 'I wonder what's going to happen to her
marriage now? No wonder she looks so depressed. What a
terrible time she's having. First her husband wants a divorce
and now Mama is so ill.'

'We live so near to each other in London. I'll do what I
can to comfort her,' Lizzie promised.

It was at eleven o'clock that night, shortly after everyone
had gone to bed, that the housekeeper was asked by the nurse
on duty to inform everyone that Her Ladyship was suffering
from another attack of cardio failure and that the family should
go to her bedside quickly.

'Laura, is that you?' Catriona asked in a small but calm voice
as Laura entered the darkened room, lit only by candles.

'Yes, darling, I'm here,' Laura replied, stretching forward to
put her arm around Catriona's shoulders.

Their mother was propped up by pillows as she struggled
to breathe, gasping frantically for air. The doctor was standing
on the other side of the bed, looking grim as he felt her wrist
for her pulse.

'I've given her the medication which has worked in the past
but her pulse is very weak. I think she'll fall asleep in a little
while.'

The room was full by now as her daughters and sons-in-law
gathered silently around the bed. Georgie was weeping silently
and Shane had his arm around her, while Robert was holding
Diana's hand. Beattie, Lizzie and Humphrey stood at the foot
of the bed while the youngest two, Flora and Alice, stood on
either side of the Reverend Colin Maitland, who would
conduct his mother-in-law's funeral.

The doctor slipped out of the room, signalling the nurse to come with him.

'I think we should wait outside to let the family say their goodbyes in private,' he whispered to the nurse. 'There's absolutely nothing more I can do.'

She nodded in silent understanding. The moment of death should be a private matter.

The funeral of Margaret, Countess of Rothbury, was, in contrast, a very public affair. The aristocracy of Scotland and England attended, the wreaths and bouquets of flowers overwhelming the small local cemetery of Lochlee Church, where she was to be buried within sight of Lochlee Castle.

The sisters, all in black, were the last to arrive in the packed church. Apart from their many friends, the people of Rothbury had turned up as well to line the short route from the manse to St Mark's and the family were expected to acknowledge their presence. Beattie clung to Lizzie's arm, a wan and lonely figure, with Humphrey following.

Suddenly Beattie felt her other arm taken in a strong grip. A second later she found herself looking into Andrew's face, but set in a much-altered expression, miles away from the arrogant and boastful man she knew so well. When he spoke, his voice was filled with humble regret and his whole demeanour was earnest.

'Please allow me to escort you on this very painful occasion,' he said softly, offering her his arm. There was a silent pause and Beattie looked into his eyes. When her mother had died five nights ago she'd cried all through the small hours, not only grieving for the mother she'd lost but because there was no one beside her to comfort her in her hour of need.

'Thank you,' she said politely as she took his arm.

At precisely ten thirty the next morning Mr Stuart McTavish, Lady Rothbury's lawyer, arrived at the manse to read her Last Will and Testament. All the family had assembled in the drawing room and the atmosphere was relaxed now that the funeral was over. Andrew and Beattie sat together on a sofa while the others hid their surprise that he was there at all. Laura sat next to Catriona, who was the worst affected by her mother's death and kept dabbing her eyes with a lace-edged handkerchief.

Mr McTavish opened his briefcase and extracted several sheets of paper, pinned together and covered in small, neat writing.

'Can I ask exactly when Lady Rothbury made this will?' Humphrey inquired.

'And you are?' Mr McTavish insolently asked, annoyed that his big moment was being stolen from him, especially by an Englishman.

'I'm Humphrey Garding. I'm married to Lady Elizabeth.'

'Lady Rothbury made this will in October of last year, Sir Humphrey. Now, may we continue?' he asked with a touch of sarcasm.

Robert's eyes twinkled. 'By all means.'

Mr McTavish started to read in a flat voice. 'I hereby revoke former wills and testamentary dispositions made by me. I appoint my son-in-law Robert Lord Kelso and my son-in-law Sir Humphrey Garding as joint trustees of this my will herein after called my trustees.' There was a pause and then he started listing the eight sisters and what had been bequeathed to them. Paintings, antique furniture, jewellery, valuable books, furs and silver was to be scattered among them all and the look of horror and shock on Catriona's face was increasing with every bequest. The contents of her home were about to be spread among her seven sisters and she'd find it robbed of everything she held dear.

Worse was to come. Mr McTavish was only warming up, relishing the drama of the situation.

'The manse is to be sold outright . . .'

There were gasps of shock and Catriona turned pale.

The lawyer paused, then continued. 'The money raised by the sale of the house together with the money in my bank account is to be evenly divided between three of my daughters who have not got the support of rich husbands. The beneficiaries from the sale of the manse, and the Countess of Rothbury's personal funds plus the sale of unwanted furniture and other artefacts are to be equally shared between Lady Laura Leighton-Harvey, Lady Flora Fairbairn and Lady Catriona

Fairbairn. The sum they should each receive should be substantial enough for each of the beneficiaries to buy modest houses for themselves and acquire the standard of living they were brought up to expect.'

Mr McTavish adjusted his spectacles and looked at the assembled family.

Robert was the first to speak. 'Quite right too,' he said stoutly. 'Our wives will all be looked after by us. It's right that Laura, Flora and Catriona should be looked after.'

'Mama knew what she was doing. What a splendid will,' Humphrey echoed. 'It is the unmarried girls who need financial support. It's obvious she gave the whole matter a great deal of thought.'

'I'm so glad,' Shane exclaimed. 'I was always worried about the future, when you get too old to work,' he added, looking frankly at Laura. 'And Flora can't go on teaching for ever. This provides for the three of you and it'll make you feel secure.'

Flora nodded. 'It's wonderful of Mama to make this provision for us.' She turned to Catriona. 'Aren't you thankful that you don't have to remain in this dismal old house for the rest of your life?'

'Not really,' Catriona replied in a small voice. 'It's my home.'

'Your real home, our real home, was Lochlee Castle. You've only been here for ten years and it's so gloomy,' Flora argued. 'Now we can buy lovely cottages and do them up how we want. I can't wait.'

Laura sat listening to them and their different attitudes to the future. For her it was like a dream and as soon as Caroline's season in pantomime was over she could tell everyone what she'd been secretly planning for some time. Lack of money had prevented her from going ahead and now she privately thanked her mother from the bottom of her heart for making a dream come true.

Andrew was not going to be left out of praising his mother-in-law. 'What a remarkable lady she was.' He turned to Beattie. 'And what wonderful daughters she had too.' Beattie smiled politely but remained silent.

Only Catriona seemed upset. 'Where shall I go?' she kept saying. 'I thought I'd always stay here for the rest of my life.'

Diana and Robert immediately offered her a home with them, and Georgie suggested she live in one of Shane's pubs.

'You'd make a fine barmaid,' Shane told her. 'The punters would love you and you're still young. You might even meet Mr Right,' he added jovially.

Catriona shuddered. She never wanted to get married. The things that went on in a bedroom between married couples both terrified and disgusted her.

'I don't think so,' she cried, before bursting into noisy tears as she ran out of the room.

'Shane, you great lummock!' Georgie scolded. 'Can't you see she's still upset? She's always been sensitive and she'd hate working in a pub. She's led a very sheltered life, you know.'

'Too sheltered,' Flora observed regretfully. 'In the past I've offered her the chance to work in the school. She speaks fluent French thanks to the French governess we had but she refused, saying she had to stay at home to look after Mama, although there are plenty of servants here.'

'She'd have meant as a companion,' Diana pointed out gently.

'All the more reason why she should get off her backside now and do something interesting with her life,' Georgie retorted.

'Catriona is fragile because Mama has just died. She needs time to adjust. We've all got families to go home to. She has no one. Mama was her life from the moment she was born until six days ago. It's going to take time for Catriona to get used to that.'

'I wish she'd come and stay with us,' Diana said.

Alice, the quiet one in the family, looked at her husband. 'Look, Colin and I live a few minutes' walk away. We'll make a point of calling to see her every day, and she can come and have lunch or supper with us several times a week. As you say, what she needs is time to process this. And we'll be here to offer her support if she needs it.'

'Absolutely,' Colin agreed. 'We'll take care of her and she'll be in our prayers.'

There were murmurs of gratitude from the others. Beattie rose from her chair, saying, 'I'm going out for a little walk. Does anyone else feel like getting a breath of fresh air?'

Before anyone could answer, Andrew jumped to his feet with alacrity, saying, 'I'll go with you, Beattie. Look, the sun's shining! Let's go.'

The family watched them leave in silence, inwardly speculating what the future held for them but knowing that as Beattie's family they would give her their support no matter what.

Spring was approaching and the garden surrounding the manse was about to become a bower of daffodils and apple blossom. Lady Rothbury had loved the garden more than the house and she'd placed benches here and there so she could sit and admire the displays of flowers that flourished in the harsh Highland climate.

As they walked side by side in silence, Beattie turned to Andrew. There was something she needed to know. It had been on her mind ever since he'd turned up on the way to the church the day before. In fact, it suddenly mattered enormously, and his answer could change everything. It had kept her awake for most of the night and now she had to know.

'Andrew, did you go to her funeral?'

He looked stunned by the question and a shadow passed over his face.

'Her family banned me from coming anywhere near them, and they most certainly didn't want me at the funeral. They accused me of being an absolute rotter. And they were right.'

There was a pause and, looking up at him, Beattie saw his grey eyes were over-bright. 'They tore me off a strip,' he continued painfully, 'and blamed me for ruining her life and all sorts of other brutal things which I fully admitted to. Beattie, my darling, I behaved shamefully towards you, but if you feel you can take me back, I'll swear on our children's lives that I will never even look at another woman. It will never happen again. It was an utter moment of madness on my part which I bitterly regret. Can you forgive me? I still love you, and I'd like nothing more than to stay with you for ever.'

Beattie looked steadily at him, saying nothing herself but listening to what he had to say and wondering if her feelings towards him would change.

Andrew continued in a low voice, 'I know how much I hurt you. I know I deserve to be shunned for ever by your entire family, but if you have it in your heart to forgive me I'll do everything within my power to make you happy, because I love you, Beattie.'

'Everything is happening so fast, Andrew, and Mama's sudden death has been such a shock. I'm not sure what I feel about the future. I need time. I can't take it all in, just like that.'

'I understand, and losing your mother is a terrible shock. You can take as long as you like and I can only live in the hope that we'll be a couple again.'

That night Andrew slept in the dressing room again and left at dawn to catch a train back to London, saying he had an important business meeting to attend.

The next day the sisters started making arrangements to return to their own homes. Laura in particular was anxious to get back to see if Caroline was all right. Diana and Robert wanted to get back to their children but Catriona was delaying them by refusing to go and stay with them.

'How can I possibly leave here?' she demanded in panic-stricken tones. 'I've got to arrange for all the paintings and the things Mama left you to be taken to all your houses. Then there are masses of boxes full of papers to be sorted out. It's going to take months just to clear all the drawers in Mama's desk,' she added breathlessly.

Beattie looked at her sympathetically. 'Dearest, Mr McTavish will do everything for you.'

'But there are things I have to see to myself,' Catriona replied.

When they were alone, Laura and Diana looked at each other anxiously. Laura was the first to put into words what Diana was thinking. 'She's obviously upset about leaving here and will do everything to delay her having to move out,' Laura whispered. 'I must say, I feel awful that three of us are benefitting from her being turfed out of her home in this way.'

'Catriona is not the only pebble on the beach,' Diana protested. 'I think Mama was right to leave the bulk of her money to the three of you who have no one to support you. What would you do when you can no longer work? And Flora, too. In the end she's benefitting as much as you and Flora so it's very fair. I know it's hard for her right now because she was so close to Mama, but Mr McTavish will look after all the arrangements.'

'If she'll let him,' Laura remarked drily.

'I'll get Robert to tell him to look after everything,' Diana said firmly. 'I have a feeling that she was expecting to be left this house and all the contents for the rest of her life,' she added thoughtfully.

Laura looked appalled. 'Do you really think so? How lonely she'd be in a ten-bedroom house! And think of the expense of paying the staff wages? She can't really have expected that, can she?'

Diana shrugged. 'I don't envy Mr McTavish. I fear he'll have a battle on his hands, and to allow her to stay here at vast expense for the rest of her life would have been really unfair to you and Flora.'

Edinburgh, 1920

Laura was surprised to find the flat as neat and tidy as when she'd left it the previous week. Caroline was notoriously undomesticated and she'd feared that she'd return to a hovel of dirty dishes and untidiness. She smiled with delight. Then she took her suitcase into the bedroom they shared and for a moment her heart stood still with shock.

It was exactly as she'd left it and she could see from the way she always folded over the top sheet that the bed hadn't been slept in. So where had Caroline slept? And who with? Like her mother she'd been brought up to believe that it was immoral to sleep with a man until the wedding night.

'Men talk,' Lady Rothbury had told all her daughters. 'If they meet a girl who will sleep with them they will tell all their friends and in no time at all that girl will have a bad reputation. Even if she's only slept with one man she'll never get a decent husband.'

Laura and all the others had listened and obeyed Mama. It was important to find a 'decent husband'. In fact, it was vital unless they wanted to end up spinsters. Mama was right, Laura reflected now. Robert, Humphrey, Shane, Colin and even Andrew would never have married her sisters unless they'd been virgins. When she married Walter she was still a virgin, despite being engaged to Rory.

If Caroline . . . At that moment she heard a key in the lock and Caroline came bouncing into the room.

'Oh, you're back?' she said, surprised.

'Yes, I'm back,' Laura replied evenly. 'Where have you been staying while I was away?'

Caroline flushed, her face red. 'With one of the girls in the show,' she replied defensively.

'Where does she live?'

'What is this? The Spanish Inquisition?'

'I asked Mrs Anderson to keep an eye on you. Have you seen her?'

'Oh, that old bag! She popped in the first evening and I thought she'd never go. I was meeting Charlotte for supper and when I eventually got there Irene said I could sleep at her place. Ask her if you don't believe me,' she added rudely.

Laura sank into a chair. 'Caroline, my mother has just died. The funeral was two days ago. I am tired and upset. I want to believe you but somehow I don't. Haven't I always told you the most valuable possession a young woman can have is a good reputation?'

Caroline looked sulky but her eyes brimmed with tears. 'I did stay with Charlotte,' she insisted. 'In the boarding house where she's staying.'

'Are there young men staying in this house, too?' Laura asked.

She nodded. 'It's full of people from the show.'

'But you slept in Charlotte's room instead of coming home?'

Caroline nodded again. 'I'm so sorry about Granny. Was it a big funeral?' It was obvious she was trying to change the topic of conversation.

Laura had suddenly had enough. Tired and deeply saddened by Mama's death, the tears ran down her cheeks. She'd returned to Edinburgh longing to tell Caroline they would be receiving a lot of money when Mama's affairs were settled but the moment wasn't right. For a minute, she felt defeated. Caroline had always been a handful and now she was a young woman the struggle to keep her from getting into trouble was going to be considerably more demanding. Walter had indulged her when she'd been small and as far as he was concerned she could do no wrong.

'I'm going to have a rest,' Laura said, fighting back tears.

'What about supper, Muzzie? I'm starving,' Caroline said in a helpless little girl voice.

'You seem to be able to look after yourself so why don't you make your own supper?' Laura walked out of the room, averting her face, overwhelmed by what had happened in the last few days and filled with dread for the future. How had this come to pass? she asked herself as she lay down.

London, the next day

As the Rolls-Royce drew up outside the imposing Belgravia house, Beattie turned to Lizzie and Humphrey with a smile of gratitude. 'My dears, I can't thank you enough for everything. The journey to Scotland and back would have been a nightmare without your help.'

'Darling, it was nothing,' Lizzie replied, while Humphrey pointed out Beattie's luggage to their chauffeur.

The sisters kissed goodbye. 'Good luck, Beattie,' Lizzie whispered. 'Whatever decision you make, you know that I'm here for you.'

Beattie had told her about Andrew wanting them to stay together and that she still hadn't decided what to do.

'I'll keep you posted,' she whispered now. 'It's a big decision.'

Humphrey escorted Beattie up the white marble steps with a discreet, 'Take care of yourself, my dear.'

'I will. And thank you again for everything. My! It's been a strange week, hasn't it?'

'And a sad one. We shall all miss Mama.' He squeezed her hand before hurrying back to the car. She watched his retreating back. He'd been wonderfully forgiving when Lizzie had had an affair. Was she as generous-minded as him? Would she ever forgive Andrew and act in such a noble manner?

The first thing she noticed about the house was that there were great vases of roses in every room.

'Where did they come from?' she asked Briggs, the butler.

'Mr Drinkwater ordered them, milady. He knows they are your favourite flowers.'

'The children are at school, I imagine?'

'Yes, milady. Can I get you anything? A cup of tea or coffee?'

'No, thank you, Briggs. We had breakfast on the train. I think I'll go to my room and have a little rest. Is my husband at home?'

'No, milady. He left early but he asked me to tell you that he'll be home for dinner tonight.'

'Thank you, Briggs,' she said lightly as she climbed the wide ornate staircase.

Beattie saw it as soon as she entered the bedroom and her pulse quickened. A large, flat leather jewel case had been placed on the pillow of her side of the bed. Striding across the room she picked it up with trembling hands. Sitting on the side of the bed, she opened it. 'Dear God!' she said under her breath.

On a shaped bed of black velvet lay the most exquisite diamond necklace she had ever seen. The stones had a fiery glitter and in the centre of the case were a pair of drop diamond earrings in a design that matched the necklace.

She couldn't help but be hypnotized by the sheer beauty of Andrew's present. Conflicting thoughts raced through her mind. Was Andrew buying her forgiveness? Then she thought how wonderful it would look the next time they went to a Royal Family gathering. But of course if she got a divorce there would be no more invitations to grand functions. An hour passed and by now she was lying on her bed with the open jewel case by her side. Mesmerized by the magnificent jewels she rolled over and started laughing quietly to herself. If Humphrey had forgiven Lizzie (despite her never even apologising for her behaviour), then she could certainly forgive Andrew.

Leaving her bedroom, she went down to the kitchen where she ordered Andrew's favourite dishes to be served at dinner that night.

'For the first course, Mrs Clark, can you make prawn cocktails, followed by lamb cutlets with all the trimmings and then meringues filled with cream and a hot chocolate sauce?'

'Yes, milady. Would you like it served at eight o'clock as usual?'

Beattie looked thoughtful, and then she turned to Briggs. 'Can you put a bottle of our best champagne on ice and serve it in the drawing room at eight o'clock, please.' Then, turning to Mrs Clark, she added, 'We'll dine at eight thirty.'

'Very good, milady.'

When Beattie had gone they looked at each other triumphantly. Their jobs looked safe. The chambermaid who had cleaned and made up the bed with snowy sheets had reported in excited whispers that 'Mr Drinkwater 'asn't 'alf got some jewellery for 'er Ladyship. If that don't work nuffink will,' she'd added in her cockney accent.

Later in the day, Kathleen and Camilla returned home from their lessons at Miss Dunlop's School for the young children of the nobility.

'Mama!' they shrieked with delight when they saw Beattie. She hugged them in turn, her eyes brimming with tears at the reminder that her own Mama was no longer with them.

'Was Grandma's funeral sad?' asked Camilla.

'Hush!' reprimanded Kathleen. 'Daddy said we weren't to talk about that because it would upset Mama.'

Beattie pulled herself together and put her arms around them. 'That was very kind of Daddy,' she told them. 'It is very sad and we'll all miss her very much but life goes on. What did you do at Miss Dunlop's today?'

They all started talking at once and the tremulous moment had passed. She just wished that her mother had lived long enough to know that she planned to stay with Andrew.

By seven thirty that night she'd put on an elegant black dinner dress with long sleeves and a low V-neckline. Then she put on the diamond necklace. It was colder and heavier than she'd expected, and a moment later the matching earrings hung from her lobes. Looking in the mirror at her reflection, the effect was dazzling. Her heart was beating with excitement when she heard knocking on her bedroom door.

'Come in, Andrew,' she said gaily. This was the moment she'd been looking forward to all day.

It wasn't Andrew. Briggs stood in the doorway, his face pale.

'I'm sorry, milady. The police are here. There's been an accident.'

She could feel the blood draining from her face and her head began to ache. 'No . . .' she croaked feebly.

'Mr Drinkwater was on his way home and a large lorry crashed into his car . . .'

Her hands flew to cover her face. 'No! No!' she beseeched. 'I'm afraid . . .'

'No! It can't be . . .'

Briggs kept control of his emotions. 'Mr Drinkwater has been taken to Saint George's Hospital and there's a police car downstairs ready to take you to the hospital. I'm afraid his chauffeur was killed instantly.'

Beattie was tearing off her jewellery and, grabbing a coat, she struggled into it as she followed Briggs down the stairs.

'I can't believe this is happening,' she whispered. 'Not now. Not when . . . Briggs, the children mustn't be told until we know how badly my husband has been injured.' Her voice caught on a sob of pure panic.

'I'll look after everything, milady.'

The Manse, earlier that day

Catriona looked at Mr McTavish in bewilderment. 'What do you mean? Mama's will very clearly lists what she's leaving to my sisters, and only then do we have to sell this house.' Her voice was surprisingly firm.

'Your late mother's will at no point stresses the order in which her property is to be disposed of,' he pointed out firmly.

'In that case why don't we give what she has bequeathed to my sisters first? You must understand I'm in no hurry to move. There is so much to sort out and I can't do it in a matter of months. I need several years before the house can be sold.'

Mr McTavish had always viewed Lady Rothbury's youngest daughter as meek and mild; an inexperienced woman who had lived a sheltered life as her mama's companion. It was therefore a surprise to find himself up against a stubborn spinster who disagreed with everything he said. Maybe he was handling the situation in the wrong way? Maybe he should appear kinder and more paternal.

'Look, my dear,' he began in what he hoped was a calm and patient manner, 'you and the other two beneficiaries of the sale of this house want to raise as much money as you can. Right now you'd get a really good price. But strip it of the paintings and furniture and the price will drop dramatically. You'd need to have every room redecorated to cover the markings on the walls where pictures were hung, then you'd need to get new drapes for the windows because these ones will look shabby against fresh paint. You will spend a fortune to get it to look as good as it does right now.'

Catriona looked at him stony-faced. 'Why can't we leave things as they are for a while? My mother has only just died and, as I have said, I'm not in a hurry to . . .'

'Nevertheless, your sisters are. Lady Laura and Lady Flora asked me when could they hope to buy houses for themselves. My job, Lady Catriona, is to carry out Lady Rothbury's wishes as speedily as possible. I will be putting the house in the hands of Fraser and Scott, who are top-rate estate agents. They will evaluate the worth of the house and aim to find a suitable buyer.'

Catriona gazed out of the window, her expression bleak. 'So that's that then,' she said quietly, as if defeated. 'Why did you let my mother make such a complicated will?' she asked bitterly.

The lawyer looked surprised. 'It's not complicated, really. You don't have to do anything except sort out your mother's papers, but only if you want to. I can do that for you, and I'll make all the arrangements with the estate agents.' His tone became even more gentle and sympathetic. 'Once the house has been sold I'll also arrange for the items she bequeathed to your sisters to be sent to their houses. And I can arrange for the remaining furniture and paintings to be auctioned; that is, if you and Lady Laura and Lady Flora don't want them for the houses you intend to buy for yourselves.' He rose to leave and she followed him to the front door, wondering when this nightmare was going to end. Ever since Mama died, the horror of what was to happening was overwhelming her. Everything she loved and valued was being torn away. What did she think that morning before Mama became ill? Probably that she'd be alive for another ten years or so. After all, she was only seventy-six, and what did she think would happen then? She imagined that she'd continue to live there, cherishing everything in memory of her beloved Mama. She'd have two more Cavalier King Charles spaniels to go with Max and Lottie and they would be her family. Dogs were so much easier to look after than children and, as far as she could see, far more rewarding.

Catriona reached for the phone. She would talk to Robert and tell him that he must get hold of Mr McTavish and insist things be left as they were for the foreseeable future. What was the hurry? She mentally put her foot down. From this moment, she refused to even consider moving out.

London, that night

It was two hours since Beattie had arrived at St George's Hospital but the nurses kept saying she could see her husband as soon as he came out of the operating theatre.

'Is he badly injured?' she kept asking, but the nurses always side-stepped her questions by telling her the surgeon would be able to tell her in due course. It was eleven thirty, too late to get a message to Lizzie – too late to get anyone. Supposing he dies? Supposing he's already dead?

At that moment, a tired-looking man in white overalls came hurrying along the corridor, accompanied by a nurse.

'Mrs Drinkwater?' he inquired, and Beattie jumped to her feet. 'How is my husband?'

'He's going to be fine. He has some broken bones, particularly to his right leg and shoulder, but we've pinned him back together and I don't expect any complications. He'll have to stay here for several weeks but he should make a complete recovery in time. He's forty-two and his general health seems good, so I don't expect any problems.'

Beattie nodded wordlessly, hardly daring to believe that Andrew would be making a full recovery. As a wave of relief washed over her, she said, 'Can I see him now?'

'Yes, but he'll be a bit woozy so it would be best to only

stay with him for a few minutes. The nurse will take you to see him now.'

'Andrew?' she said softly once the nurse had led her to his bed. His face was grey and drawn and his eyes were closed. 'My poor darling. I'm here and I'll always stay by your side,' she whispered.

His eyes opened. 'You mean it?' he murmured.

'Yes, I mean it. I was going to tell you tonight. I'd ordered your favourite dinner as a thank you for the beautiful necklace and earrings.'

'You like them?'

'I love them, but more than that, I love you.'

'Mrs Drinkwater, your husband needs to rest. Why don't you come back tomorrow?'

Andrew frowned. 'She's Lady Beatrice Drinkwater.'

Beattie smiled. She knew her title meant a lot to him but she didn't mind. He was her husband for better or worse, and for that she was now enormously thankful.

Dalkeith House, four months later

'You need a rest, sweetheart,' Walter told Caroline as she yawned and stretched her arms above her head. The show had come to an end and this was the first weekend they'd been free to visit her father.

'I've got to get another job,' she pointed out. Her tone was martyred.

'That's what I want to discuss with you both,' Laura said.

They looked at her and Caroline retorted, 'What is there to discuss? Neither of you know what it means to be a ballerina.'

'There's no need to be rude,' Walter said, but his tone was hopelessly indulgent.

Laura took a deep breath. 'I shall be coming into quite a bit of money in a few months' time. And you and I,' she added, looking at her daughter, 'are going to leave Scotland. To begin with we'll be staying with Aunt Lizzie, who has very kindly said she'll have us to stay while I look for a flat. There's one thing I know about being a great ballerina, Caroline, and that is that London is the place to be. There's Saddler's Wells, Covent Garden and a wealth of theatres. Perhaps Madame Espinosa could recommend a good London agent to find work for you.'

Caroline flung her arms around her mother and her face was radiant.

'That's perfect! It's just what I need, isn't it, Dada? To live in London! I can hardly believe it! It's like a dream come true! Where is the money coming from?'

Laura could see that Walter was pleased for Caroline's sake but it was obvious that he was going to miss her.

'You must come and stay with us, Walter,' Laura said, smiling at him. 'The money is from what your grandmama left to me. The manse has also been sold and the money is to be split three ways between Aunt Catriona, Aunt Flora and me so that we can buy homes of our own. Nothing grand, mind you. I'd like a flat but I expect my sisters will get cottages.'

Rowena entered the room and Caroline made her mother repeat her wonderful news.

'Isn't it exciting?' Caroline kept saying. 'When are we going to London?'

'These things take time,' Laura explained, 'but Mr McTavish is seeing to all the arrangements.'

'Why just the three of you? What about the rest of your sisters?' Rowena enquired.

Laura hesitated slightly, and then spoke with care because she knew Walter was listening. 'My other sisters have no need for money so Mama felt Catriona, Flora and I needed to be looked after. I think Mama decided that as the three of us have to earn our own living, we should get a helping hand. Everyone has been left something in the way of antiques, silver, paintings and jewellery so everyone is happy.'

'That's very fair,' Rowena remarked.

Walter nodded. 'Extremely fair. I'm so happy for you, Laura. God knows you deserve it.'

'Will you give up dressmaking?' Rowena asked.

Laura shrugged. 'I don't know. We'll have to see. Living in London will be a lot more expensive than Edinburgh.'

Walter suddenly rose and walked out of the room. Rowena

and Laura exchanged looks and Caroline was now immersed in the theatre reviews of *The Scotsman*. If Rowena's expression showed that she considered Laura's treatment of Walter was ruthless, Laura felt no embarrassment. Instead of sponging on her rich sisters she'd worked night and day to provide a home, food on the table and even ballet lessons for Caroline.

The Manse, a month later

With every passing hour Catriona's feelings of anguish and anxiety increased. Bit by bit the house was being stripped of its paintings and antique furniture that had been a part of her life since she'd been born.

The family portraits in heavy gilt frames no longer gazed down at her, the landscape of the Isle of Mull which had hung over the study fireplace, the exquisite painting of a Madonna and Child; all gone to hang in the homes of Diana, Beattie, Lizzie and Georgie. Catriona wondered if they would love them as she had loved them. She was filled with sorrow for the loss of this dear old house that had sheltered Mama and her for so long.

The now-blank walls had grubby marks where the paintings had previously hung, giving the whole house an air of forlorn abandonment that broke her heart.

The once-cosy study and the elegant drawing room were cold and half-empty now. The exquisite French marquetry cabinets with shelves displaying Dresden china figurines had gone, and so had the side tables on which had stood priceless *objets d'art* of great value and beauty. Mr McTavish had been right when he'd insisted the manse should be sold in all its glory.

The new owner, a businessman from Glasgow, had offered to purchase what was left in the way of furniture, including the four-poster bed, because they were 'classy'.

'Before I agree, do you or your sisters want to keep anything special?' Mr McTavish had asked Catriona. She'd wanted to scream, 'It was all special! Every stick and stone of it!' But she'd bitten her bottom lip and shaken her head in silence.

'I suppose most of it is too big for a country cottage or a

London flat,' he said, trying to lighten the desolate atmosphere that now pervaded the manse. 'Have you found a smaller house for yourself?' he added.

'I've looked at a few,' she replied vaguely.

'Time for a new start!' he continued bracingly. 'The staff here seem to be very happy that the MacAndrew family have asked them to stay on. Very happy indeed.'

She had avoided talking to them about the drastic changes that were underway, knowing she would break down, and Mama had always told her never to let a servant see you cry because it was inappropriate.

'Yes,' she whispered, knowing she would never be happy again. She'd lost her mother, her home and everything in it. The future was a blank page. Taking a deep breath, she said, 'Thank you, Mr McTavish, for all your help, your thoughtfulness and your kindness.'

He blinked in surprise. 'Thank you, Lady Catriona. It has been a very difficult time for you and your family and I'm sure you're glad that we have carried out the wishes of the late Lady Rothbury.'

Catriona reached out to shake his hand. 'Can you do one last thing for me?' she asked unexpectedly.

He raised his bushy eyebrows in surprise. 'Certainly. What would you like me to do?'

'Can you tell all the servants that they can take today off? They needn't return until late. Tell them I'd like to be alone to say goodbye to the house.'

He bowed to her in an old-fashioned way. 'Your wish is my command, Lady Catriona,' he said, smiling. 'I'll go and tell them right away. I'm sure they will be delighted.'

As soon as he'd left the room, Catriona clutched her chest, and, staggering towards the window, buried her face in the dusty silk of the curtains, stuffing the fabric into her mouth and biting down hard so her sobs wouldn't be heard. The despair was unbearable. 'Mama, how could you do this to me?' she moaned. The house seemed very quiet now so she hurried into the hall and climbed the stairs to what had been her mother's bedroom. There was her four-poster bed, which now belonged to Mr and Mrs MacAndrew.

Flinging herself down on the counterpane, she lay there for a long time, hoping for solace and comfort as her mother had shown her when she'd been a child, but now there was only coldness and terrifying loneliness.

There was no consolation. As she lay there, she realized the pain would never go away.

Struggling to her feet, she left the room and climbed to the floor above where the spare rooms were, and then up another flight to the attic where the servants slept. Breathless and aching with tiredness, she managed to unlock a hatch that led on to the flat, lead-lined roof.

The sun was shining and there was a warm breeze that ruffled her hair and chilled her face and hands. Surrounded by mountains of purple heather, her eyes were stinging as she gazed at the magnificent view for the last time. This was the only way to stop the pain.

Stepping forward, her fists clenched in determination and her mouth set in an expression of grim resolve, she jumped.

Cranley Court, the next morning

News of the tragedy reached Diana and Robert first when Mrs Durrant, the housekeeper at the manse, phoned them at dawn to say the staff had all returned to the house after dark and had presumed Lady Catriona had gone to bed. She paused as if she didn't know what to say next.

'Right,' Robert said uncertainly. He was standing in the hall wearing a silk dressing gown over his pyjamas, having been woken up by the butler. 'What can I do for you, Mrs Durrant?'

Her words came out in a hysterical rush. 'I've just found her body on the terrace. Frozen stiff, she is.'

It took a moment before Robert understood what she was telling him. 'Mrs Durrant . . . Please . . . please explain what you are trying to say.'

'She's gone, sir. Dead. What – what shall I do?'

'Phone the police immediately. Don't touch the body and don't let anyone touch anything else either. That's very important.'

'I ken the poor wee bairn has done away with herself,

milord,' she stammered tearfully. 'She gave us all the day off yesterday and told Mr McTavish that she wanted to be alone to say goodbye to the house. I ken she planned what she was going to do.'

'I'm afraid it sounds like that. My God, this is terrible. You must try to keep calm, Mrs Durrant. Get on to Mr McTavish and ask him to come to the manse. He can deal with the police. My wife and I will drive over as quickly as we can but it will take several hours.'

'Thank you, milord. Will you tell Lady Laura? I ken they were close.'

'I'll inform them all. Don't worry.' Robert replaced the telephone earpiece on its hook and raced up the staircase to where Diana was still asleep.

'Di?' he said softly as he entered the room. 'Wake up, dearest.'

'What is it?' she asked dozily.

'Bad news, I'm afraid, my darling.' He sat on the edge of the bed and reached for her hand, hating every moment of what he was about to do. 'Terrible news and you're going to have to be very brave.'

'The children . . .?' she asked fearfully, instantly alert.

Robert shook his head. 'It's about Catriona.' He watched a shadow cross her face but forced himself to continue. 'They found her lying on the terrace this morning.'

'Oh, God, not again,' she cried out.

'What do you mean?'

'Our younger sister, Eleanor. She had a terrible accident when we lived in Lochlee Castle. She fell out of her bedroom window while trying to lift a curse that had been put on our family.' Diana wept.

Robert had heard about the accident, or suicide, as it was widely thought to be by the public, before he'd met the Fairbairn family.

'I'll never forget seeing her poor little broken body on the terrace. And now Catriona. It's like we're still cursed.' She covered her face with her hands in a gesture of utter despair and began to cry softly into her hands.

'I don't think this was an accident,' Robert said carefully, trying to prepare her for the worst.

Diana dropped her hands and looked at him. 'What? You think Catriona committed suicide?'

'It looks like it. I've told Mrs Durrant to tell the police and Mr McTavish. I'm so sorry, my darling. I told her we'd drive over right away, but I've promised to tell the others so I'll do that while you get dressed.'

Diana had gone white as a sheet and she struggled to speak. The tears silently ran down her face as she thought of her sweet, quiet little sister who had only wanted to be left alone in the manse. 'I'll . . . I'll phone my sisters. I should do it.' She shuddered at the prospect.

He put his arms around her and held her close. 'I'll do it, sweetheart. You've got enough on your plate and it's going to be a very long day.'

Diana nodded, unable to speak. Robert was always so good in emergencies and a tower of strength that she could fall back on at a time like this.

One by one he relayed the shocking news to Lizzie, Beattie and Georgie, discovering when he got through to Alice and Flora that they had already heard about the tragedy as they lived in the same village as the manse. He had left Laura last, terrified to bring her such terrible grief. He knew how close she had been to Catriona, and she would have no one to comfort her except her selfish and unpleasant daughter.

'I have some terrible news to tell you, Laura,' he began.

'I know,' she said furiously. 'Lizzie has just told me.' Her voice was rough and croaky, as if she'd been crying, but her tone now was sharp and full of bitterness. 'We should never have done what Mama wanted. That will betrayed Catriona. She'd forced my sister to be dependent on her and she was treated like a lap dog. Then when Mama doesn't need her any more she leaves instructions for the manse to be sold, kicking Catriona out of her home. You and Humphrey should have thrown that bloody will on the fire and let my sister stay there for the rest of her life if that is what she wanted.'

'Laura, we don't know at this stage if leaving the manse had anything to do with her wanting to end her life. I fear it was the loss of her mother that tipped her over the edge. Maybe she has left a note. It's too soon to speculate, my dear.'

'I can tell you, Robert, I don't want a single penny from Mama's estate now,' she said fiercely. 'If it has cost my sister her life to make the sacrifice of selling the manse which she loved then I don't want a farthing,' she cried passionately. 'I knew what Mama and the house meant to Catriona and I can only blame myself for being too selfish to realize how that will would destroy her.' She began to sob uncontrollably.

Robert spoke firmly. 'Laura, you must not blame yourself. Catriona was thirty-two. She had a mind of her own. She wasn't a child.'

'That's just what she was,' Laura retorted. 'A sheltered, over-protected girl who wasn't allowed to have friends of her own age because Mama feared she'd get married and leave home.'

'But Catriona was as much of a beneficiary of this will as you and Flora. Your mama wanted the three of you to be able to have your own homes with enough money to keep you comfortably off for the rest of your lives.'

Laura was trying to control her emotions and get Robert to see her point of view. 'Flora and I are different to Catriona. We don't need looking after. We earn a living for ourselves. Catriona was different. Mama purposely made her different. I can't bear to think how desperate she must have felt and not one of us was there to comfort her.'

'Will you come now, Laura?' he asked gently. 'Diana and I are setting off in a few minutes. Like you, she's terribly upset.'

'I'll be getting on the next train,' Laura replied, 'but it's too late, isn't it? It's too late.'

The Manse, the next day

'This is like a weird re-enactment of Mama's death, isn't it?' Humphrey observed in a low voice as he shook hands with an exhausted Robert as they stood in the drive. He and Lizzie, with Beattie and Andrew, had travelled overnight by train and they were being welcomed with tearful hugs by Diana, Flora and Alice, whose clergyman husband, Colin Maitland, was bracing himself to impart further bad news to the family.

'This is going to be a hundred times worse than their mother's funeral,' Robert whispered. 'All the sisters are utterly inconsolable, and Laura is as angry as hell that we didn't burn her mother's will in the first place.'

Humphrey blew his nose into a large handkerchief. 'Let's hope Mama kept a well-stocked wine cellar to help us all get through this ghastly business. Have they ascertained that it was definitely suicide?'

Robert nodded. 'A trapdoor that leads on to the roof had been forced open.'

Humphrey immediately looked up at the chimneystacks. 'God, it's a hell of a drop.'

Lizzie had seen him looking up and she came over to him with tears in her eyes.

'I'm so sorry, darling,' he murmured, putting his arms around her.

'How brave she must have been,' Lizzie said, looking up at the roof too, 'to do this. But not brave enough to face the future.'

'That was Mama's fault,' Laura pointed out as she overheard Lizzie's remark. 'We all knew she had a hold over Catriona. But none of us did anything to get her away from it all.'

'I think she'd have fiercely resisted leaving here or getting a job. She looked upon Mama and this house as her *raison d'être*,' said Humphrey.

'That's exactly what it was,' Laura declared, 'and she should have been allowed to do exactly that without interference,' she added angrily.

Flora came over to her and said, 'I hear you are refusing to accept Mama's wishes regarding the money.'

'That's right. You can have the whole of it including Catriona's share now, but I can't take a penny. I should have seen this coming but instead I sailed back to Edinburgh planning a whole new life in London, particularly for Caroline's sake.'

Flora stared at her. 'So you're going to be as selfish as our mother? If someone wants to end their life nothing will stop them. Your guilt is groundless and will cause Caroline to be denied the chance of a good career – all because of your self-ishness. Like mother like daughter. Catriona didn't want a career or a job teaching French. She didn't want friends. I tried everything to get her interested but she absolutely refused. So stop playing the martyr and think what opportunities you can offer your own daughter now.' With that she turned away and marched off to talk to Lizzie and Beattie.

Mr McTavish and the Reverend Colin Maitland were huddled in a corner of the study, deep in conversation.

'Would you like me to tell the family?' the lawyer asked.

Colin looked strained. 'That's very kind of you but I think it's my job as the village parson and a member of the family.'

'Does your wife know?'

'No. She's got no idea.' His pale face looked worried at the prospect and his hands trembled.

'Then do it now. Everyone is here, making plans and it's only fair that you should inform them as soon as possible,' Mr McTavish advised.

'You're right.' Looking grim, Colin rose to his feet and went over to where his wife was sitting. Alice looked up at him. 'What is it, dearest?'

'I have to tell everyone something very important before you all make plans for Catriona's funeral,' he replied. Robert and Humphrey overheard and there was soon silence in the room as the family looked up expectantly.

'I'm sorry to have to do this,' Colin began nervously, 'but what you don't realize is that we can't have a traditional funeral for poor Catriona.'

There were muffled gasps of surprise but before anyone could question his pronouncement he swiftly added: 'I'm afraid that a person who has taken their own life is not permitted to be buried on consecrated ground. That is what the Bible says and that's what the Church of England stands by. We're going to have to find a beautiful spot and I will do all I can to . . .'

His words were drowned by exclamations of horror and sorrow. At that moment, Mr McTavish spoke, ruling out any lingering hope they might have of laying Catriona to rest in the grounds of the house she so loved. 'I got in touch with the new owner of the manse and the extensive garden, but he refused to consider a burial here. We must think again and we must do it quickly.'

'How about the grounds of Lochlee Castle?' Robert suggested. 'The Fairbairns owned it for nearly five hundred years and Catriona was born there. Would you like to drive over now and ask their permission?'

'I'll come with you,' Humphrey offered. 'I'm sure the owners will agree and we'll pick a beautiful secluded spot.'

Three days later Catriona was laid to rest in an oak coffin not far from the fast-flowing river where she and her sisters had paddled when they'd been small and the air had been filled with only the sound of youthful laughter.

Nine

'Did you say Laura and her daughter are coming to live in London?' Andrew asked Beattie as they sat having dinner at home one evening.

'Yes. They're staying with Lizzie to begin with while Laura looks for a flat.' At that moment the butler left the room and Beattie could talk more freely. 'Thank God she changed her mind about accepting the money Mama wanted her to have.'

'I think Flora changed her mind for her,' Andrew observed, smiling. 'I overheard Flora saying she was being selfish.'

She smiled back, toying with the roast lamb and redcurrant sauce on her plate. Apart from the tragedy that had swept them all into mourning, the past year had been the happiest she'd ever had with Andrew. He was a changed man. The arrogant showing off was long gone and he'd been attentive and caring towards both her and the children.

'What's wrong with your dinner, sweetheart? You're picking at your food?' he asked with concern.

Beattie pushed her plate away. 'I'm not hungry,' she confessed.

'Do you feel unwell?'

'Not really.' Then she grinned and whispered, 'I wasn't going to say anything until I was certain, but I'm fairly sure that I'm pregnant.'

Andrew's face lit up with delight and he glanced over his shoulder to make sure they were still alone. 'Let's go up to our bedroom in a few minutes so I can show you how happy you've made me. I love you so much, Bea. You know that, don't you?'

Beattie nodded and pursed her lips as she heard the butler's footsteps coming along the hall. 'Where do you suppose Laura should look for a flat?' she asked, loudly.

He laughed and gave her a roguish look. 'In the West End, perhaps? Near all the theatres.'

'That's a good idea.' She longed for the touch of his hands and the feel of his body lying alongside hers. Then she blew him a kiss when the butler's back was turned and Andrew winked back.

'I think I'll go and rest,' she said loudly. 'It's been a long day.' She rose to leave the table. Andrew looked up at her with longing. 'I've had a frantic day, too. I'll follow you up in a minute.'

The butler scurried down to the kitchen and whispered to the cook, 'They're going to be at it like rabbits tonight. Didn't even wait to finish the main course.'

Her face fell. 'What about my chocolate soufflé?'

'Well, we're not going to be like rabbits so let's have it ourselves.'

'How long are Aunt Laura and Caroline going to be staying with us?' Margaret asked her mother.

'I'm not sure,' Lizzie replied. 'It depends how long it takes them to find a flat. I'm so thrilled they're going to be in London though, my darling. I've always been closest to Laura, perhaps because she was born fifteen months after me so I can't remember a time when she wasn't around.'

'When are they arriving?'

'The day after tomorrow,' Lizzie replied. After the terrible sorrow of the previous year she was positively excited to have something to look forward to. 'I thought we'd give a dinner party that night to welcome them. You'll be in, won't you?'

Margaret, named after her late grandmother, shrugged as she smoothed down her long dark hair. 'I don't know about the others but I will be out.'

Lizzie frowned with annoyance. 'But I want you all here and I've invited Beattie and her family. What are you doing?'

'Going out with Richard.'

'Well, on this occasion invite him here. It would be an opportunity for him to meet all your cousins. Aunt Beattie is dying to meet him too. He's such a lovely young man.' Lizzie's expression softened. 'He's so eligible, too. Meanwhile, I'll have

Laura and Caroline from going on trips, confining their travelling to visiting Walter.

The girls were eyeing Caroline now, taking in her fair hair cut short in the new fashion and her calf-length pale pink chiffon dress, designed and made by her mother. There was something about her that they knew they didn't possess. Although not a great beauty, her dark eyes flashed with gaiety and animation and Margaret had heard her mother telling someone her niece had 'star quality', whatever that was.

'I hear you're a dancer, Caroline,' Isabel said boldly.

Before Caroline could answer, Rose asked, 'What is it like to dance in front of hundreds of people? I'd be terrified.'

Camilla, who was only nine, nudged her on the arm. 'Me too!'

Caroline could see they were all a bit shy and the only person who'd chatted to her at dinner had been Uncle Humphrey.

'Do you have to practise a lot?' Kathleen wondered. 'I'm learning to play the piano and I'm supposed to practise every day.'

For the first time in her life Caroline realized her cousins were all looking up to her. She was no longer the relative who didn't live in a big house with lots of servants, who didn't have new clothes, only hand-me-downs, who didn't have dogs or her own pony. All the bitterness she'd felt as a little girl whose mother was a dressmaker rose to the surface at that moment and she suddenly felt better than the lot of them. She had talent. She was already famous in Scotland and soon she'd be famous in England.

Turning to face them all, she spoke for the first time with assurance and a beaming smile.

'Studying ballet is rather different to playing the piano.' She paused to give Kathleen a kindly look. 'You train to be a ballet dancer, like an athlete. I trained for years with the famous Madame Espinosa and she was very strict. When it came to doing the show at the Theatre Royal in Edinburgh we rehearsed until my toes were bleeding,' she added grandly.

The girls all gave a shiver and looked at each other with dismay.

'That's why one isn't nervous when one performs to a large audience. You've rehearsed so often you could do the steps in your sleep.'

To her gratification they all looked deeply impressed. 'Could you dance for us now?' Camilla asked.

'I'd have to put on my ballet points first,' she replied, seemingly with reluctance.

There was a chorus of 'Oh do, please,' as they looked eagerly at her with admiration.

Caroline looked down at the large Persian rug. 'I can't dance on carpet.'

'We can roll it back,' Isabel declared, while Kathleen jumped to her feet and opened the keyboard lid.

'I'll play for you. What sort of music would you like?'

'Something dreamy and romantic,' Caroline replied instantly, her expression transforming to sheer happiness.

'How about Beethoven's *Moonlight Sonata*? You're quite good at playing that one,' Margaret suggested with a good-natured sisterly frankness.

The girls were clustering together, giggling with excitement at the novelty of seeing someone dance in Aunt Lizzie's drawing room.

'OK. I'll do it,' Caroline said, as if she was making a great sacrifice.

'Mummy, can we roll the carpet back? Caroline is going to dance for us,' Margaret explained.

'Of course you can, darling,' Lizzie replied. 'Rose, sweetheart, can you go down to the dining room and tell Daddy to come up and bring the others,' she added. 'He won't want to miss this. Humphrey adores ballet and opera.'

While Rose scurried off the others rolled back the carpet and re-arranged the chairs so that when Caroline returned fifteen minutes later the two families and Richard, Margaret's boyfriend, were sitting expectantly in a semi-circle.

From the open doorway Caroline gave Kathleen the signal to start playing the piano. She'd decided to improvise *The Dying Swan* which she'd seen Anna Pavlova perform in Edinburgh several years ago, and which had reduced her to tears. She'd show these rich cousins how talented she was.

The lease was for seventeen years and the rent was much less than she'd budgeted for. In an unexpected stroke of good luck, the previous tenant was happy to leave a lot of his furniture behind as he was emigrating to Canada.

Laura was ecstatic, rushing back to Lizzie to give her the good news.

'We'll be moving in next week,' Laura announced triumphantly, 'and it's divine, with two bedrooms, a drawing room and a dining room, plus a nice bathroom and a very good kitchen.'

Lizzie smiled radiantly. 'That sounds perfect and it's very near to us! Oh, Laura, I'm so glad that you've found somewhere nice. I feared you'd move to one of the suburbs and we'd hardly ever see you.' At that moment her worries that Caroline would get in between Margaret and Richard vanished from her mind.

'My plan was always to find a suitable place for us in central London because Caroline has to be near the West End. There's a bus stop just round the corner that goes straight to Piccadilly.'

'What's the address?'

'Eleven, Emperors Gate,' Laura said with pride. 'I can't wait to tell Caroline. It's time she had a proper home and a room of her own.'

'Will you take up dressmaking again?' Lizzie asked.

Laura shrugged. 'It depends on a lot of things. If Caroline becomes very successful I'll have my hands full because she'll need to be chaperoned, especially if she tours.'

'So really her career becomes in part your career? My God, I couldn't do that. Will she pay you from what she earns? If I were going to dedicate my whole life to one of my children I'd expect to be paid.' She spoke seriously.

Laura shrugged again. 'She's my life, Lizzie. Ever since Walter and I separated Caroline has been my life.'

Lizzie remained silent. That was the problem. Caroline took her for granted. She never acknowledged that sometimes her mother had stayed up all night finishing a garment for a customer who needed it by tomorrow. No one could say Laura hadn't been a devoted mother but in doing her duty she had indulged Caroline into thinking the world must revolve around her and her alone.

'Don't act like you are jealous,' Lizzie warned Margaret. 'It might give Richard ideas.'

'I hate her,' Margaret declared bitterly. 'Why did you let them come here in the first place? Aunt Beattie could have put them up.'

Lizzie didn't reply. Beattie had told her in confidence that she was expecting another baby, but it was early days and she didn't want anyone to know yet.

While Caroline was having meetings with her new agent, who had been recommended to her by Madame Espinosa, Laura went on a spending spree to get things for their new flat. It was already basically furnished but her aim was to get it looking perfect before Caroline saw it. Her pictures, crockery, cutlery and of course her sewing machine were being brought down by Carter Patterson, but in the past she'd never been able to afford the small luxuries that enhance a room. She went to Whiteleys, a big store in Bayswater, where she bought table lamps with pretty shades, attractive rugs to place on the existing carpet, soft cushions, a large mirror to hang above the mantle shelf and a nice desk. Most important to her, she then added to her list of shopping a large sofa that opened out into a bed. She wanted to be able to invite Diana, Georgie, Alice or Flora to stay; they could bring their husbands and have her room and she could sleep in the drawing room. As a final touch of elegance she also bought several vases that she planned to fill with flowers when she took Caroline to see her new home; the first proper home she'd had since she'd been a small child. Laura glowed with pleasure at the thought. To be able to provide everything that Caroline needed had been her aim all along.

Ten

Diana and Robert were sitting by the fire reading the newspapers after dinner when Diana exclaimed, 'Goodness!'

He gazed at her fondly. 'What is it, darling?' They were thankful to be on their own after a hectic Christmas and the New Year hosting Flora, Alice and Colin, and Georgie and Shane with their badly behaved children, Jock, Ian and Harriet. Relishing the peace and quiet that filled the house, they'd decided they would take Archie and Emily, who were grown-up now, for a skiing holiday over Christmas the following year.

'Listen to this,' Diana told her husband. 'Outstandingly talented Caroline Harvey, the protégé of Madame Espinosa, will be taking the lead role in a new ballet, *Rainbows*, at the Sadler's Wells Theatre, opening on March the third.'

'Good for her,' Robert remarked.

'Do let's take a trip down to London so we can be there. Also, Laura has been inviting us for ages to stay with her in her flat. I think she's longing to return some hospitality.'

'Pity Georgie doesn't think along those lines,' he grumbled.

Diana laughed. 'That's because they know we'd hate sleeping over a pub, amid the fumes of ale,' she replied soothingly.

'All right,' he said amiably. 'On one condition, though.'

'What's that?'

He gave her a roguish smile. 'The condition is that we go to a suite at the Ritz secretly the night before we go to Laura's so that I can have my wicked way with you!'

Diana leaned back in her chair, overcome with laughter. 'You do that anyway! Remember in the woodshed in the forest? And in that cave on the side of the mountain?'

Robert was laughing too. 'Hush! The children might hear you.'

Diana spoke softly. 'Robert Kelso, you're a very naughty boy but I do love you.'

'I know,' he said quietly. 'Do you fancy an early night?'

'You know I always fancy early nights,' she whispered, gazing into his eyes.

London, 1922

As Caroline came out of the Barons Court rehearsal rooms in West Kensington he was waiting for her. He'd been waiting for her for the past week because rehearsals took place during the day when none of her family would be with her. Once *Rainbows* opened her mother would be chaperoning her every night and meeting in secret was going to be more difficult.

'Hello, Richard,' Caroline exclaimed as if she was surprised to see him. She noticed he was wearing a smart navy pinstripe suit with his trilby hat and he carried a rolled umbrella. She smiled with approval.

'Hello, Caroline. How are you? How did it go today?' he asked as his strong blue eyes swept over her from her slim ankles to her bright little face. 'Would you like to go to Gunter's for tea? We can get a cab and be there in ten minutes,' he added with boyish enthusiasm.

'What about being seen?' she asked anxiously. She wasn't sure whom she feared most if she and Richard were seen together: Margaret or her own mother?

'It will be all right,' he said recklessly. 'We'll sit at the back in a corner.' At that moment a cab appeared and he hailed it with a wave of his hand.

Caroline loved the masterful way he did everything with great confidence, as if he owned the world. She'd heard her mother and Aunt Lizzie agree he was a 'great catch' and she'd made up her mind that he would be her catch. He could afford to take her to all the best restaurants and he'd promised her that one day they would go to the Savoy for dinner and dancing to a famous band under the glitter of crystal chandeliers in the ballroom.

Enthralled by the life Richard led, Caroline realized what she'd been missing, living in a small flat in Edinburgh and so poor they could never afford to go anywhere. Margaret had always lived in style and took it for granted; now it was her turn to smell the roses. All she needed to do was to make Richard fall deeply in love with her.

Richard reached for her hand and squeezed it as the taxicab rattled along the busy streets of London, and she had never felt so happy. For the past two weeks they'd been so careful not to be seen together but now she didn't care. Margaret had to realize that Richard was no longer her boyfriend, and as far as she was concerned, the sooner the better. Caroline had overheard Aunt Lizzie tell her mother that the romance had never gone further than kissing and her mother had replied, 'Of course not,' because a well-brought-up young lady would never permit it. It left Caroline wondering what she should do if Richard wanted more than a kiss? Girls had to be virgins on their wedding night.

When they arrived at Gunters she realized it was terrifically smart and the chance of seeing people he knew was high. High-ceilinged and spacious with a large window overlooking Park Lane, they were ushered to a table in a discreet corner. Caroline was in her element. She chose toasted teacakes, cucumber sandwiches and creamy meringues from the pink menu which matched the pink tablecloths, and her eyes sparkled as she looked at the fine white and gold china crockery. It was all a world away from the little café that she and the other dancers frequented.

'You're hungry,' Richard remarked fondly as she ate the toasted teacake.

'I'm always hungry,' she admitted. 'I work so hard for hours on end and then realize I'm starving.'

Richard leaned forward. 'Will you come out to dinner with me one evening? We could go to the Café Royal.'

'My old-fashioned mother doesn't allow me to go out on my own; it's got to be in a group. She's very strict.'

'Even if the man is trustworthy?' he persisted.

'But . . .' She paused, not wanting to offend him. 'You are Margaret's boyfriend.' Her mouth suddenly drooped at the corners and it looked as if she was about to burst into tears. 'We're just friends, aren't we?'

He looked appalled. 'But I don't feel about Margaret in the same way as I do about you.'

'Does she know that?'

'I think she realized,' he said quietly.

Over the years, Caroline had learned not to push people too hard, so she dabbed her mouth with the pink napkin and gave a sad little subdued sniff. Richard reached out and placed his hand over hers.

'It's you I care about,' he said softly as he looked into her eyes.

That evening, when she got home later than usual, she found her mother in an agitated state.

'Where have you been?' she asked. 'One of the other dancers phoned to speak to you. Apparently rehearsals finished this afternoon? What have you been doing for the past two hours?' Laura asked anxiously.

'This is not my prison, you know,' Caroline retorted, throwing her bag on to the sofa, 'though it feels like it.'

'I was worried about you. You don't know your way around London and it can be a dangerous place to go wandering around alone.'

'I wasn't alone!' her daughter snapped back furiously.

Laura looked at her calmly, fully aware that Caroline was hiding something. 'So who were you with?'

Caroline's pale face flushed scarlet. 'It was Richard Montgomery, if you really want to know.'

There was silence. 'Did you bump into him?' Laura asked politely.

'He's in love with me. He's been waiting for me every day and today he took me to tea at Gunters,' she boasted. 'Then he paid a taxicab to bring me home.'

Laura looked apprehensive. 'Gunters, of all places,' she murmured. 'He must have taken you there on purpose. Lizzie and Margaret will probably have heard by now and they're going to be absolutely furious with us.'

'Why angry with you? It's me they're going to want to kill,' she added triumphantly. 'It serves Margaret right for being such a cow to me ever since we were children. She always looked down on me for not living in a proper house with

Caroline's expression became sulky. 'I can look after myself.'

'They all say that,' Robert declared, 'until they've had their handbag stolen or something much worse.'

'That's very kind of Irene's mother to say she'll get you a taxi,' Laura said calmly. When they were alone she'd tick Caroline off for the underhand way she'd asked for permission to go to a party, knowing her mother would agree to avoid a scene.

The next morning Diana and Robert bid Laura goodbye, saying how much they'd enjoyed their stay. It was only when they were alone in the taxi as it sped in the direction of Piccadilly that Diana said, 'I feel awfully guilty for pretending to Laura we were going to Paris.'

Robert chuckled. 'Well we are. Tomorrow.'

She looked at him. 'What do you mean?'

'We're staying at the Ritz again tonight in their best suite. But I know how you hate lying, so we're going to Paris tomorrow, where I've booked another suite at the George VI hotel.'

Diana looked excited but at the same time agitated. 'But . . .?' she began.

'Don't worry.' He patted her hand. 'I've got our passports; the children know and so does everyone back at home. Apart from making you an honest woman as far as Laura is concerned, I thought you needed a bit of fun. You've had a very tough year with both your mother and Catriona dying.'

Diana's face was flushed with emotion. 'I'm the luckiest woman in the world to be married to you,' she said breathlessly. 'I'd no idea . . . does Laura know we're going on to Paris?'

'Yes. She was very amused.'

'I do hope she's not lonely in London, what with us leaving today and Caroline going to a party this evening.'

'I don't suppose so. At least she's got Lizzie and Beattie only a short distance away,' Robert assured her. 'I've booked a table in the Ritz's restaurant for eight o'clock this evening and I thought we might have a look at a new exhibition in the Royal Academy this afternoon.'

Diana closed her eyes for a moment as the taxi rattled past

Green Park. 'I hope this isn't a wonderful dream that I'll wake up from in a minute.'

Robert squeezed her hand. 'If it is I'm having the same dream,' he whispered.

Rehearsals were over for the day and all the dancers had congregated in one of the larger dressing rooms, where they could do their make-up and change out of their leotards and pink tights into pretty dresses, stockings and evening shoes with Louis heels. Shrill voices were asking each other what they were doing because this was their last evening of being free to go to parties. Soon they'd be performing until ten o'clock, by which time all they'd want to do was crawl exhausted into bed.

'What are you doing tonight?' Caroline was asked over and over again. They were filled with curiosity about this girl from Scotland who referred to her mother as Lady Laura and said she'd been born in a grand castle. She'd got this far, they concluded, because she'd obviously spent a fortune being trained by Madame Espinosa, and now Lady Laura had obviously 'pulled strings' to get her daughter a starring role. In short, she was viewed as an outsider whom they didn't much like.

'I'm just going out to dinner,' she replied casually. In twenty minutes Richard would be waiting for her outside the stage door and she wasn't sure where he was taking her, nor did she care. One thing was certain: she wasn't going to Irene's birthday party because Irene didn't exist. If her mother wanted to meet 'Irene' one day she'd say she'd left the company.

'You do look lovely,' Richard said as soon as she emerged from the theatre.

'Do I?' Her tone was arch.

He held open the waiting taxi door for her to step in.

'Dover Street,' he said briefly to the cab driver as he got in and took his place beside Caroline.

'Where are we going?' she asked, crossing her legs and admiring her beautifully shod feet.

'My flat. I've been in Dover Street for the last five years. It's in walking distance to my club, which is very convenient.'

Caroline decided that she would never let her mother know

she'd gone alone to a man's flat. Echoes of Laura's warning words spun through her mind. 'It looks bad even if nothing happens,' and, 'If someone saw you coming out your reputation could be ruined.'

Then there was the other warning. 'Men talk. If you sleep with one man and he tells his friends . . .'

All this was going through her head as the taxi shuddered along as other thoughts, her own this time, were thinking, *I want to encourage this man to fall in love with me and even marry me . . . how can I make a fuss about going to his flat? I bet Margaret's been to it dozens of times . . .*

'Here we are,' Richard announced as they stopped outside an apartment block.

Am I doing something really stupid? Caroline asked herself as she looked up at the building. *But what else am I to do?*

'What would you like to drink?' Richard asked as she sat in one of his armchairs.

The voices in her head started again. *Don't accept alcohol. There's nothing worse than a drunk woman. Men will take advantage of you if you're drunk.*

'A cup of tea would be lovely,' she replied meekly. He looked surprised but went to his small kitchenette and finally brought her tea and a little plate of sweet biscuits.

'I think it's time we had a serious talk, Caroline,' he said, drawing up another chair for himself. She waited silently but her heart was hammering and she felt certain he was about to say Margaret's parents were expecting him to marry her and that's what he felt he should do.

'You sound very serious,' she said crisply, and her eyes glinted angrily. She had never hated any one as much as she hated Margaret at that moment.

Richard continued, 'I am serious, I can assure you. I've known Margaret for the past eighteen months and I believe she's in love with me and expects me to propose.' He paused and looked troubled.

Caroline got to her feet. 'Fine. Why don't I just go now? You're obviously regretting leading me up the garden path so I'll spare you any more embarrassment by going,' she snapped pettishly.

Richard looked horrified. 'What are you talking about? It's you I'm in love with.'

'But you've just said . . .' She tossed her head as she started to walk out of the room. Grabbing her by the wrist, he looked into her eyes and saw not arrogance but fear.

'Listen to me, Caroline,' he said commandingly. 'What I said was that Margaret seems to expect me to propose to her, but it's you I'm in love with. From the moment I saw you dancing in her parents' house I've only thought about you. If I marry anyone it's got to be you, my darling.'

Caroline's expression changed to one of elation as she impulsively threw her arms around his neck. 'I love you, too.'

Richard led her to one of his big armchairs and she sat on his knee like a little girl while they talked about the future.

'Tomorrow I'll go to see Margaret and tell her that our romance is over,' he said.

'Will you tell her that you're in love with me?' she asked.

Richard's eyebrows rose. 'I don't think that would be very diplomatic,' he replied. 'In the course of time it will be obvious to her and everyone else that I love you but in the meantime let's not make it worse for her. She's a very sweet girl and I don't want to hurt her if I can help it.'

Caroline felt a pang of disappointment. She'd have given anything, *anything* to have let Margaret know immediately.

'So where are we going to celebrate tonight?'

He kissed her lightly on the lips. 'I've booked a table at the Ritz, sweetheart.'

'What an amazing menu,' Diana remarked as they sat making up their minds what to order. They'd been given a table by the window overlooking Green Park and she'd murmured, 'How romantic.'

'I think we should start by ordering champagne, don't you?' Robert pointed out.

'That would be heavenly.' Diana sighed, gazing up at the painted ceiling where golden cherubs held up garlands of flowers.

'I'd forgotten . . .' she began, then giving a gasp she exclaimed, 'Oh, no!'

Robert turned round to see what had caused her dismay but she whispered, 'Don't look round, Robert.'

'Why? What is it?'

Diana's mouth tightened. 'That little minx! She asked Laura's permission to go to a friend's birthday party, and here she is wineing and dining with a young man. Laura will be furious.'

'Only if we tell her,' Robert pointed out. 'Has she spotted us?'

'No, she's far too full of herself. Anyway, we said we'd be in Paris; remember?'

He nodded. 'Let's keep it that way. Laura won't thank us for letting the cat out of the bag and Caroline will hate you for ever.'

Their champagne had arrived and he raised his glass. 'Here's to us, my darling! We're far more interesting than a young girl who's managed to get a rich young man to take her to the Ritz.'

Diana raised her glass. 'Thank you for twenty-six years of married bliss, my love,' she whispered.

'Let's forget them,' Robert said. 'They apparently haven't seen us.'

'That's because she has her back to us. He's facing this way but of course he doesn't know I'm her aunt,' Diana pointed out.

As they made their way through Whitstable oysters, roasted goose, Isinglass blancmange and lobster croque, Diana seemed to have forgotten Caroline and her young man until Robert suggested they go to bed in order to get up early to go to Paris. As they were leaving the restaurant, Diana darted over to where Caroline was sitting with Richard.

'Hello, Caroline. Fancy seeing you here? I thought you were going to Irene's birthday party.'

Caroline looked as if she was going to faint for a moment, then she blushed a deep red.

'Change of plan,' she muttered, totally unprepared for this intrusion.

Richard had got quickly to his feet, smiling but looking confused. There was a moment of deathly silence before Caroline remembered her manners. 'This is Richard Montgomery. My aunt, Lady Diana Kelso and my uncle, Lord Kelso.'

'How do you do,' Richard said politely as they shook hands. Diana's face had hardened when she heard his name. 'Then you know my sister, Lizzie Garding and her family, don't you?'

'I do, indeed. You're very alike.' It was obvious Richard was embarrassed and Robert was murmuring something about wanting an early night before they set off for Paris. Diana stared coldly at her niece. 'Goodnight,' she said formally as she followed her husband out of the restaurant.

'I've a good mind to telephone Laura,' she fumed as they entered their suite. 'I should also warn Lizzie that her wretched niece is trying to nab Margaret's boyfriend.'

'You'll do nothing of the kind, Di. Let them sort it out themselves,' Robert said firmly.

Diana turned to look at him as they entered their bedroom where the soft pink lighting had been left on, the enormous bed with its pink satin eiderdown had been turned down and the air was heavily scented with the perfume of great arrangements of roses.

'But Caroline is obviously after Margaret's boyfriend and she's lied to Laura about what she's doing tonight. Lizzie told me that Humphrey is expecting Richard to go to him and ask for Margaret's hand in marriage,' she protested.

'Darling, it's not about our daughter, thank God. I don't care who Caroline run's off with and you shouldn't care either. I promise you, if you interfere both Lizzie and Laura will turn on you. For goodness' sake, don't meddle.'

'I know you're right but I feel I'm letting them down by not warning them about what's going on.'

Robert put his arms around her and held her close. 'You're not letting them down, sweetheart,' he murmured softly. 'If we'd gone straight to Paris we'd never have seen them. Remember we lied, too, by saying we were going straight to Paris. We weren't supposed to be in this hotel. Caroline got the shock of her life.'

Diana gave a little chuckle. 'Good,' she exclaimed. 'I hope she was frightened out of her wits.'

'How about another drop of champagne before we go to bed?'

'That would be perfect,' she whispered.

★   ★   ★

Laura heard Caroline's key in the lock of the front door shortly after eleven o'clock.

'Hello, darling,' she called out. 'I'm about to make a cup of hot chocolate. Would you like one too?' Delighted that her daughter had come home at a reasonable hour, she was surprised when Caroline came rushing into the room, looking distraught.

'Oh, Muzzie, I'm in terrible trouble and I don't know what to do.'

'What sort of trouble? Were there young men at Irene's party?'

Caroline flung herself on to the sofa and she looked scared. 'Irene's party? No, I didn't go to that. I went to the Ritz for dinner . . .'

'Who took you there?' Laura was immediately worried. Caroline was very gullible and her mother had visions of her going up to a man's room and being assaulted.

'Richard took me,' she retorted, angry that her mother always jumped to the worst conclusions. 'He's going to end his romance with Margaret and he's in love with me. Aunt Diana was very nasty to me when she realized . . .'

'What's it got to do with Diana?'

'Will you listen, Muzzie. Aunt Diana and Uncle Robert were also having dinner at the Ritz . . .'

'Stop talking nonsense. They left for Paris earlier today,' Laura retorted.

'Will you listen to me? They were at the Ritz and I just know Aunt Diana is going to get in touch with Aunt Lizzie and she's going to kill me!'

Laura sat down again, looking perturbed. 'How long has this being going on?'

'What does that matter? Richard is always hanging around waiting for me to come out of the rehearsal rooms. It's not my fault,' she added belligerently.

'You could have reminded him that he was Margaret's boyfriend and has been for over a year.'

Caroline took off her high-heeled shoes and tossed them carelessly away. 'He's planning to tell her it's over between them. We went to his flat to talk it over before going to the

Ritz . . .' Too late, Caroline realized she had let her mouth run away with her.

'You what?' Laura exclaimed. 'How many times have I told you . . .'

'Yes, yes,' Caroline said impatiently. 'I've heard it all a thousand times. "Your virginity is your greatest asset". Richard and I just talked and then we went to the Ritz for dinner. How was I supposed to know we'd bump into Aunt Di and Uncle Robert there? I don't want another lecture about making sure I have a spotless reputation. I need you to stop all the bloody aunts from having a go at me for going to a restaurant with a very nice and eligible young man,' she shouted furiously.

Laura turned pale with anxiety and her head was beginning to ache. 'Does Aunt Lizzie know that Richard is interested in you?'

'Not yet, but she soon will.' Caroline looked smug. 'He's going to tell Margaret tomorrow. Oh! I'd love to be a fly on the wall. She's going to be absolutely furious with me.'

'I knew he admired your dancing but I thought he'd have the decency not to pursue you. Why on earth did you encourage him?'

Caroline sat upright with an expression of astonishment. 'Don't tell me that when you were young and an eligible, good-looking young man took an interest in you, you didn't respond?'

Laura paused, thinking back to when she'd been seventeen and Rory Drummond, who was handsome, had come to a ball given by her parents at Lochlee Castle and they'd fallen in love on that magical night. Rory had made it clear there and then that he was unattached. Three months later they were engaged.

'Well?' Caroline broke into her thoughts.

Laura spoke without hesitation 'No decent man would take up with a girl while still being on the verge of getting engaged to another girl. Margaret is your cousin and both you and Richard are guilty of deceiving her. If he's genuinely in love with you he should have kept away from you while he ended it gently with Margaret, so it wouldn't look like he dumped her for you.'

Caroline laughed. 'This isn't eighteen twenty-two!' she retorted. 'And I'm delighted he's dumping her for me.'

Laura's mouth tightened. 'You have many faults but I didn't think crass cruelty was one of them.' Then she strode out of the drawing room and went to her bedroom, slamming the door behind her, feeling a mixture of anger laced with tears of disappointment.

Beattie was resting on the chaise longue in the drawing room now that she was entering the last few weeks of her pregnancy, when Lizzie's arrival was announced.

'My dear, I don't want to disturb you,' she began as she sat down on a nearby chair. 'I'm so sorry to barge in like this but I thought it unwise to telephone you to tell you what's happened.'

'My dear Lizzie, it's so nice to see you. I'm bored to death having to rest so much because the doctor says my blood pressure is rather high. What new excitement have you got to tell me?'

'It's not excitement; it's a tragedy,' Lizzie retorted.

'Why? What's happened?'

'Richard came to see Margaret this morning to tell her he's ending their romance.' She reached for her handbag and pulled out a lace-edged handkerchief with which she dabbed the tip of her nose. 'Margaret is heartbroken, as you can imagine. Oh! I'd so hoped he was going to marry her.'

'My goodness, that's very sudden, isn't it? Hasn't he been wineing and dining her as usual?' Beattie asked.

Lizzie looked thoughtful. 'I suppose he has but he's been sort of different. Margaret said to me earlier in the week that he seemed distant and moody.' Her eyes brimmed with tears. 'My poor baby. She's so upset.'

'I'm sure she is. It's a fearful blow. I wonder if he's met anyone else? That's what usually causes a relationship to break up, and I should know,' she added meaningfully.

'Is everything all right with Andrew now?'

'He's being an angel, kind and considerate and very happy about the baby. He's hoping it will be a boy, of course, but he never says so.' Beattie smiled. 'I'm quite excited myself and so are the girls. Whatever it is, it's going to be utterly spoilt by everyone.' She sounded content and Lizzie envied her for a moment.

'I must leave you, my love, but I wanted you to know what had happened.'

'Are you going to see Laura?'

'Yes. She met Richard when she and Caroline were guests in our house,' she added bitterly. 'It never crossed my mind that Caroline would steal him from Margaret.'

'I was there. I remember Caroline danced beautifully,' Beattie added. They looked at each other, then Lizzie spoke in hollow tones.

'Do you think that was the moment when . . .? Richard was very taken by her dancing . . . Oh! Surely not?'

Lizzie rose briskly. 'There's only one way to find out. I'm going to see Laura and ask her outright if Caroline has been seeing him since that first night.'

'Why didn't you tell me what was going on?' Lizzie demanded, her grey eyes flashing with anger as Laura felt bound to confess that Richard had taken Caroline to dine at the Ritz, where she'd bumped into Diana and Robert.

'I had no idea she'd met Richard until she came home last night.' The two eldest Fairbairn sisters, born only fifteen months apart, had always been close, but now there was a chasm of distrust and ill-feeling between them.

'I had no idea until last night that she was friends with Richard Montgomery,' Laura repeated in protest. 'From what I can gather he's been turning up and waiting for her outside the rehearsal rooms. She could hardly be rude to him,' Laura protested. It was the truth but, nevertheless, she felt guilty and Lizzie knew it.

'So who told him where she was rehearsing? Margaret doesn't know where it is so the information obviously comes from the horse's mouth.'

'Will you stop accusing Caroline and me in this way,' Laura retorted indignantly. 'I don't believe the address of where they're rehearsing is a state secret,' she added sarcastically.

By now the sisters were sitting glaring at each other.

'You've no idea what a state Margaret is in. She's in love with Richard and she'd set her heart on marrying him,' Lizzie said with bitterness. 'It really is too bad that your minx of a daughter has stolen him away.'

'She's not a minx and one supposes that Richard is a grown man who can pick any girl he wants. If he is a rotter isn't it better Margaret knows about it now instead of after they were married?'

Lizzie paid no attention to what her sister had to say and became even more furious. 'Just because her father is a bankrupt alcoholic you've overcompensated and ended up making her a thoroughly spoilt little brat! I, for one, will never forgive her for breaking Margaret's heart. Did we try and steal each other's boyfriends when we were young? No, our mother taught us better manners.' Lizzie rose. 'I can see myself out.'

When she'd gone Laura burst into tears. Had she really been such a bad mother? Was Caroline the selfish, grabbing little minx that Lizzie declared she was? Did she still indulge and spoil her daughter? It was true she wanted the best for the only child she'd had and yes, she would love her to marry well but never at the cost of cheating or stealing a cousin's boyfriend. She'd done her best to support Caroline; she'd worked night and day to make enough money to send her to ballet school but now, suddenly, it all seemed to have gone wrong. She'd fallen out with Lizzie and her other sisters would criticize her for pampering her daughter at the expense of others. The first night of *Rainbows* was in a week's time. Would all the family come to the premiere? Somehow she now doubted it.

Eleven

London, 1922

Beattie reached to turn on the bedside light as her heart pounded with fear. 'Andrew?' she cried out.

Her husband woke up immediately. 'What is it?'

'I'm bleeding badly and I've just had a contraction.'

Andrew knew the baby wasn't due for another month and this had never happened with their three other children. Panic seized him as he sprang out of bed. This was exactly what had happened to Beryl Cooper and she hadn't only lost their baby, she'd lost her life.

'I'll call for an ambulance. Just lie there. Don't move.'

He dashed from the room and hurried down the stairs to the telephone on the hall table, muttering under his breath, 'Please God, don't let this happen again. Haven't I been punished enough? Oh, God, please take care of Bea and the baby.'

Up in the bedroom, Beattie was saying her own prayers and trying to keep calm. As soon as the ambulance arrives everything will be all right, she assured herself. At that moment she had another severe contraction and the flow of hot blood increased, frightening her.

Andrew came rushing back to the room. 'They'll be here in a few minutes, darling. I'm just going to put on some clothes so I can come with you.' Disappearing into his dressing room he grabbed trousers, a tweed jacket and a pair of shoes.

'I'm scared,' Beattie whispered as he walked over to the bed to hold her hand. Her face was very pale and there were dark shadows under her eyes. For the first time she looked very frail and vulnerable.

'Would you like me to get Laura or Lizzie to be with you, sweetheart?'

She shook her head and gritted her teeth as another

contraction gripped her with agony. When it passed she sobbed, 'It's never been like this before. Perhaps I'm getting too old to have babies.'

The same thought had crossed Andrew's mind but he said robustly, 'Too old? Nonsense my darling! You're not old at all.'

At that moment they heard the ambulance arrive.

'Thank God! I'll run down and let them in,' he exclaimed with relief, while Beattie lay there hoping it wasn't too late.

Laura awoke at four o'clock in the morning, roused by her sixth sense and a bad dream. Instantly alert, she climbed out of bed intent on making sure Caroline was all right. Now they had separate bedrooms she often awoke in alarm because there was a new fear now: was her daughter alone? Was it possible that once she'd gone to bed Caroline might slip out to meet Richard at some secret rendezvous or, worse still, allow him to creep into her bedroom?

With bare feet she padded down the corridor and opened the door silently. Caroline lay curled up, fast asleep, and Laura instantly felt a mixture of relief and guilt. How could she not trust her beloved daughter? She'd been strictly brought up and Laura felt ashamed of not trusting her now she'd reached the age of eighteen.

She climbed back in to bed but a heavy premonition still hung over her. Deciding it was just the lingering result of a disturbing dream, she went back to sleep.

Lizzie was still wide awake, fretting over Richard having dropped Margaret in favour of Caroline. How could he have been such a bounder? Just when she'd thought her second-youngest daughter had a secure future with the right kind of husband. It was time Isabel came out and was presented at court and she'd need to find a husband, too.

It was going to cost Humphrey a fortune to bring out his daughters and the expense didn't end with balls. There were the clothes and hats for going in the Royal Enclosure at Ascot, then there was Goodwood, Henley and a hundred other balls to attend. Her thoughts were interrupted when she suddenly heard the telephone ringing down in the hall. Who on earth could be ringing them at two in the morning?

Flinging a shawl around her shoulders, she hurried down the stairs to the hall. Something told her it could only be bad news and she thanked God that at least Humphrey and the girls were all safely home and asleep in their beds.

The white marble hall floor felt icy beneath her bare feet as she reached to lift off the earpiece.

'Hello?'

'Oh, Lizzie! We're at Saint George's Hospital – Beattie is desperately ill.'

She recognized Andrew's voice and he sounded frantic. She'd never liked him much with his boasting and bragging about how much money he'd made, and she'd found it hard to forgive him the affair he'd had with his secretary, but now she felt desperately sorry for him.

'My dear Andrew, I'm so sorry. Has the baby been born yet?'

'No, but it won't be long now. The trouble is Bea's haemorrhaging badly – something to do with the placenta – and her heartbeat is irregular.' His voice trailed off and she heard him sob. 'I'm so afraid she isn't going to make it.'

Lizzie's own heart froze. 'I'll come right away so you're not on your own,' she said, trying to keep her own voice steady.

The nurse hurried towards Andrew with a little bundle in her arms. 'You've got a beautiful little boy, Mr Drinkwater,' she said as she put the baby in his arms.

Andrew looked down at the pink, crumpled tiny face and then looked up at the nurse. 'How is my wife?'

There was a fraction of a pause before she answered but he knew she was making an effort to keep the calm expression on her face. 'The doctor is with her now.'

At that moment Lizzie came hurrying along the corridor, followed by Humphrey. It was obvious they'd quickly put on day clothes over their nightwear.

'What a beautiful baby,' Lizzie whispered while her husband patted Andrew on the shoulder, murmuring, 'Well done, old chap.'

Andrew nodded, unable to speak as silent tears ran down his cheeks.

'How is Beattie?' Lizzie whispered nervously.

Andrew shrugged, holding the baby tightly to his chest, unable to answer.

'I'll see what I can find out,' Humphrey told them reassuringly as he shuffled off, his pyjama top showing above his tweed jacket and his hair ruffled from sleep. Lizzie watched him with gratitude, loving him more at that moment than she'd ever done. A nurse came hurrying towards them but she'd come to take the baby off to be washed and dressed.

'You can see him when he's in the nursery with all the other babies,' she told Andrew. When they'd gone he covered his face with his hands in a gesture of sheer despair.

'Beattie will be all right.' Lizzie tried to sound positive. 'We're a very strong family, Scottish born and bred, and she'll be absolutely delighted she's had a little boy. Your son and heir, Andrew.'

Then they saw Humphrey walking quickly towards them. Beside him was a figure dressed in the white clothes of a surgeon.

'Mr Drinkwater?' he asked as he neared Andrew and Lizzie.

Andrew nodded as if bracing himself for the worst.

'Your wife has had a very nasty time but I'm delighted to tell you she's out of danger. We've managed to stop the haemorrhage but she's very weak and needs a lot of rest. I'd like her to stay in the hospital for a couple of weeks to regain her strength.'

It was as if a ten-ton weight had been lifted from Andrew's shoulders, and as he shook the doctor's hand he thanked him profusely.

'You've got a fine little fellow, too. There's nothing the matter with him. Now, Mr Drinkwater, you can see your wife, but only for a few minutes.'

Andrew was prepared to agree to anything, he was so thankful.

Lizzie smiled, light-headed with relief too. 'Give Beattie my love and tell her I'll come to see her in a day or so.'

'Thank you both for being here,' Andrew replied. 'I don't know what I'd have done without you.'

As Humphrey and Lizzie drove home, he said, 'When you get to know him he's not such a bad fellow, is he? There is a genuine man underneath the showing off.'

'Yes, and he certainly loves Beattie. I'm glad now they're still together.'

'When you think about what's happened it's absolutely true that God moves in mysterious ways.'

This wasn't the way Laura had expected Caroline's ballet debut in the famous Sadler's Wells Theatre to be. Beattie was still in hospital recovering from her near-death ordeal and Lizzie and Margaret still held a grudge about Richard, so the whole family had decided to stay away. Diana and Robert were unwell with bad influenza. Further north, Georgie was pregnant and Shane was nervous of her travelling as she'd suffered a bad miscarriage with her previous pregnancy. That left Alice and Colin, but he was conducting a wedding and a funeral that week and Flora couldn't get away from the school where she worked. When Walter telephoned to say Rowena wasn't well and would be unable to come Laura began to feel there was a family pact to shun Caroline's first night performance.

'But you're coming?' she asked sharply.

'I wouldn't miss it for the world,' he assured her warmly. 'I've booked into a hotel round the corner from Emperors Gate.'

'You must stay here as you're on your own. You can have my room and Caroline will be thrilled when I tell her you're staying with us.'

'That would be very nice.'

When she'd said goodbye it suddenly struck her that she was going to be escorted by a handsome man on this auspicious occasion and it was a refreshing thought after years of going everywhere on her own. All her sisters except Flora took it for granted that they'd be accompanied by their husbands, something she'd missed more than she realized, especially at her mother's and Catriona's funerals.

Now, with a light heart, she started planning what she was going to wear. No one in the stalls would know she was the lead ballerina's mother, but she knew and was bursting with pride at the prospect.

'Dada is staying with us when he comes to London,' she told Caroline.

The girl's face lit up, her brown eyes shining and her wide smile radiating beauty. 'How did you manage that? Where's Aunt Rowena going to sleep?'

When Laura had explained she wasn't well Caroline clapped her hands. 'What a bit of luck!' she crowed with delight.

'That's a nasty thing to say.'

'Muzzie, don't pretend you like her. She's always hated me and the only reason I'm sorry she's not coming is she'll miss my moment of success. I don't think she thought it would ever happen.'

'I'm thinking of wearing my sapphire-blue lace dress with the matching velvet coat I made. I might get a new pair of satin evening shoes dyed to match.'

'But nobody's going to look at you,' Caroline scoffed.

'Your father will,' Laura replied with a smile.

The applause was thunderous and several members of the audience jumped to their feet as Caroline, representing the sun in a golden costume and headdress, posed on her points centre stage with her arms outstretched. Surrounding her a dozen ballerinas twirled around in their costumes which were made of wide ribbons which floated as they moved, each one reflecting the many colours of a rainbow.

After a moment they lined up and, led by Caroline, made low curtsies to the ecstatic audience. Laura felt her throat contract and her eyes brim with tears of pride. Beside her Walter was clapping and shouting 'Bravo,' and then Laura spotted Richard two rows in front of them. It was obvious he'd brought a lot of friends and was laughing and also yelling, 'Bravo.'

Caroline had warned her mother that the performers were having a party after the performance but she wouldn't be late and the company manager had hired a charabanc and would make sure all the dancers got home safely.

'I'm going to take you to dinner at the Café Royal,' Walter told Laura.

This was a surprise she hadn't expected, and as they climbed into a taxi Laura was reminded of how he'd taken her out all those years ago in Edinburgh when he'd been a well-off retired army officer before becoming a successful businessman who'd then ruined his health and his life with alcohol. He hadn't had a drink now for nearly fifteen years and tonight it struck Laura that he'd once again become the man she'd fallen in love with. Witty and highly educated, she found herself responding and they were soon laughing in a way she never did when she took Caroline to stay at Dalkeith House. It made her realize that Rowena had a dampening effect on the conversation, apart from which she seemed to guard Walter jealously. Laura had always realized that as a widow Rowena desperately needed her brother's companionship. She always inferred that he hadn't had a drink problem before he'd married Laura, and had been able to give it up the moment she'd taken care of him in her house – something Laura had always known to be untrue.

The food was exquisite at the Café Royal and as if it was the most normal thing in the world Walter ordered wine for Laura and sparkling water for himself.

It was after midnight when they got back to Emperors Gate and Laura went to check that Caroline was home. Opening the bedroom door silently, she realized that the bed was empty.

'She's not back yet,' she told Walter, sounding anxious.

'Did you expect her to be? This is probably the biggest night of her life so far. She'll be all right, my dear. I don't think she'll be back before two o'clock. Why don't you go to bed and I'll kip down in here,' he said, indicating the sofa in the drawing room.

'No, Walter. You probably didn't get much sleep on the train last night. I want to see her anyway when she comes in,' Laura insisted. Jokingly calling her 'as bossy as ever', Walter retired for the night while Laura kept vigil, waiting for Caroline's return.

Richard was waiting for Caroline and as soon as she emerged from the stage door he rushed forward to embrace her, a handsome figure in a dinner jacket, causing the other performers who were spilling out of the theatre to look impressed.

'My darling, you were magnificent,' he exclaimed passionately. Caroline looked up at him in adoration.

'I've got a car waiting to whisk us off to the Savoy,' he said, leading her to a chauffeur-driven Daimler.

At that moment she knew this was the life she really wanted. To dance before an appreciative audience who thought she was wonderful was what she'd worked so hard to achieve. What made the moment perfect was having a rich, handsome boyfriend dance attendance on her, complete with a waiting car that would take them to the smartest hotel where one could dine and dance until two in the morning. The sheer bliss of the moment as she stepped into the luxurious pale grey suede of the Daimler made up for all the years of poverty in a small Edinburgh flat with a mother who was always tired and anxious. Now, at last, she could look her twelve rich cousins in the face as if to say, 'Look at me! And I got here by my own cleverness! You lot had it easy with your rich fathers.'

The bitterness that had seeped into her heart ever since she'd stood on the pavement outside what was no longer their house as she and her mother watched the enormous removal van drive away with all their possessions was forgotten for a little while as she smiled gaily at Richard.

'Did you get my flowers?' he asked.

'I had so many bouquets,' she lied, thinking of the bunch of roses from her mother and father, 'but yours was the prettiest of all.' And I could have bought a new pair of shoes with what it must have cost, she thought.

Although she didn't usually drink because Muzzie forbid it, Richard insisted they have champagne to go with the dressed crab, followed by roast lamb and then ice cream with hot chocolate sauce while a live band played the new popular dance music of the day.

'What divine food,' she said, scooping up the last morsel of her pudding. 'I'm more hungry than usual these days.'

'I'm not surprised,' he remarked. 'You're like an athlete in training. So much energy goes into your dancing and it shows. The other dancers look half asleep compared to you.'

'Do you think so?' she asked, pleased.

'Absolutely.'

She almost purred like a contented cat.

'Do your family know you're dining with me tonight?'

Caroline smirked. 'They think I'm at a first-night party with all the other performers.'

His face fell. 'Haven't you told them about us?'

She shrugged. 'Who I go out with is my business. I don't think they've got over the shock of hearing you chucked Margaret,' she added candidly.

'I think you ought to be honest with them,' he pointed out in concern. 'I want to be a part of your life in the future, so why can't they know about me now?'

Caroline felt rattled by his criticism. It was as if he was accusing her of being dishonest. 'My mother makes such a fuss about my going out with a man, she's a nightmare. I'm no longer a child and I can do what I like.'

He leaned forward, elbows on the table, and spoke earnestly. 'You know I'm madly in love with you and from now on I want to be a part of your life. The thing I adore about you is your independence. Your strength. Your single-mindedness. You'll go far, my darling, and I'd like to be with you as you do.'

She laughed teasingly. 'My! You're being very serious. Let's dance; I love this music.'

The band were playing a tango and she moved with a sensual grace, coming close to him one minute then swaying away the next. When Richard suggested they go back to his flat for coffee she willingly agreed. The champagne had gone to her head and she felt delightfully reckless.

Once in his flat she kicked off her high-heeled shoes and settled herself on the large sofa while Richard went into his small kitchen to make the coffee. When he returned he found her fast asleep, curled up like a small child. Her sweetness overwhelmed him and, fetching a blanket from his bedroom, he placed it gently over her, making sure her feet were tucked in. Smiling to himself, he turned off the lights and got ready for bed, thinking all the while that he was the luckiest man in the world.

A cold dawn was seeping through a gap in the blue velvet curtains of Laura's drawing room when she awoke with a start.

'Caroline?' she called out sharply as she sat up in the sofa bed.

'Hush! You'll wake up Dada,' her daughter whispered angrily, 'and before you start I went back to Daisy's house with some of the other girls after the party and I was so tired I fell asleep on her sofa. I want to get another few hours' sleep so don't let anyone disturb me.'

Before Laura could say anything Caroline had disappeared in the direction of her bedroom.

Laura lay down again, admitting to herself that she had lost control of her daughter. She was a young woman now, with a career, earning money and with a life of her own. She could be guided and advised but never again controlled. Her baby had flown the nest.

Walter appeared at that moment, wearing a tartan dressing gown over his pyjamas.

'I heard Caroline coming in and I imagine she's gone to bed.'

Laura nodded silently.

'Shall I make us cups of tea?' he offered.

'I'll do it.' Laura moved as if to climb out of bed.

'No, my dear. I'll do it. Let me spoil you for a change. I'm not helpless, you know, though Rowena seems to think I'm both hopeless and helpless.'

Laura burst out laughing. Walter had always been an amusing man with a great sense of humour and there was no doubting that his sister tried to belittle him in the eyes of others.

'Go on then. I'd love a cup of tea. No one has made me a cup of tea to have in the morning since . . .' She paused, knowing what came next.

'Before I hit the bottle too hard for the last time,' he said harshly. 'I know, Laura. I remember slipping down to the kitchen very early when we were first married to make us tea and I'm happy to be doing it again.'

Laura smiled. 'You don't have to rush back to Scotland tomorrow, do you?'

'I think I should. Rowena isn't at all well.'

Twelve

London, 1923

The smart invitation fell through a hundred letter boxes announcing the christening of Philip Martin Andrew Drinkwater at St Pauls Church, Knightsbridge, on 28 January followed by a reception at their Belgrave Square house. A separate stiff card also invited nearly four hundred guests to a cocktail party that evening at the Hyde Park Hotel.

Beattie had made a speedy recovery after her ordeal, fuelled by happiness that they'd had a boy. He was a beautiful baby too, with blue eyes and blond hair.

Henry, Kathleen and Camilla were fascinated by their little brother and Nanny Drinkwater had to put her foot down from time to time because she believed in strict routines.

'I think he's going to be fearfully spoilt,' Beattie laughingly told Laura as they had tea in the elegant drawing room which had two French windows leading on to a balcony overlooking the gardens of Belgrave Square.

Laura smiled at Beattie fondly, still feeling shaken by how near she'd come to dying. 'The most important thing is to see you so well again,' she said. 'No one deserves happiness more than you, dearest, and you've had a very tough couple of years.'

Beattie leaned forward and spoke in a low voice so they wouldn't be overheard. 'Life is strange though, isn't it? If Miss Cooper – and I shall always think of her as "Miss Cooper" – if she hadn't died and the baby boy hadn't died too, I'd be sitting here, a divorced woman, trying to bring up three daughters on my own.'

Laura nodded. 'I knew something was terribly wrong the night you were taken to hospital. I get these feelings but I never know what they mean.'

'Have you spoken to a fortune teller?' Beattie asked.

'I haven't told anyone outside the family. When it happens

I think I'm going down with influenza or something. I actually feel shivery but the strange thing is the moment I know what has actually happened I feel all right.'

Beattie looked mystified. 'That must be horrible. Did you feel like that when Catriona killed herself?' she whispered.

Laura closed her eyes for a moment as if lost in pain. 'When it happens I can feel felt quite ill and I can't think why. I'm filled with fear and sure a disaster has happened close to me, like thinking perhaps that something has happened to Caroline. London can be such a dangerous place.'

'Not when you get used to it,' Beattie pointed out. 'When I was first married I wished we lived in Scotland but now I love living here. There is so much to see and do. I hope all our friends can come to the christening. Diana and Robert are staying with us but I'm not sure about Alice and Flora.'

'I still miss being at Lochlee Castle,' Laura admitted. 'Those were the days, weren't they? What fun we had when we were young,' she added nostalgically.

'Will you go back when Caroline gets married?' Beattie asked.

Laura blinked, startled. 'Goodness, I've no idea. That's years away.'

Beattie smiled knowingly. 'I hear she's very close to Richard Montgomery.'

'Who told you that?'

'Some friends of ours saw them at the Savoy on the opening night of *Rainbows*. Apparently they were dancing cheek to cheek for half the night,' Beattie said lightly as if it was of no importance.

Laura's mouth tightened. 'A whole lot of them went out to celebrate after the show, so maybe Richard joined them,' she replied. So Caroline had lied to her. What other lies had she told? Hurt as well as perturbed, she decided to change the topic of conversation.

'What are you going to wear for the christening, Beattie?'

Her sister's eyes sparkled. 'Pale blue, of course. I love the new fashion of slim-line dresses with dropped waists and thank goodness I've got my figure back. I've got a matching coat and a pale blue cloche hat with blue roses on the side.' She extended her left hand and Lizzie saw a new ring beside her platinum wedding ring; it was a large sapphire surrounded by diamonds.

'That's beautiful,' Laura exclaimed.

Beattie smiled. 'Andrew bought two rings to be on the safe side. The other one is set with a ruby and diamond in case I had another daughter,' she added with satisfaction. 'He said I can keep it too.'

Laura had never been able to replace any of her jewellery which had been seized by the bailiffs, but she had bought herself a gold wedding ring in a pawn shop so that no one would think she was an unmarried mother.

'Darling, you must have almost as much jewellery as Queen Alexandra,' Laura joked.

Beattie laughed. 'Andrew is very generous, I must say. Sometimes I feel he's bought me. Would I have stayed with him if he'd been poor? It's an uncomfortable thought to have to admit. I really like the good things in life and I'll put up with the bad things because a big diamond here or a sable coat there would shut me up.'

'I think the real test is would you have married him if he'd been poor?'

Beattie didn't answer immediately and then she said in a small voice, 'No, probably not.'

It was a bright, crisp day for Philip Martin Andrew's christening and the high society of the day gathered at the church to see and be seen. Photographers and gossip columnists clustered on the pavement ready to note and take pictures of this society event. It was the world of the aristocracy that Andrew had cultivated and loved. The very fact that his wife was titled and the daughter of an earl never ceased to thrill him. It gave him an entrée into royal circles and he was determined to expand his charitable work so in due course the King would grant him a knighthood.

Members of the Fairbairn family gathered around the font. Caroline was in her element because they all wanted to know how *Rainbows* was going. From being the poorest member of the family she now felt like a star. Her young cousins looked at her with awe because the reviews described her dancing as 'exquisite'. The poor cousin who only had hand-me-downs was famous, much to their amazement.

Diana's children, Archie and Emily, couldn't believe that this was their little girl cousin, now a beautifully dressed celebrity. She'd been so awkward and chippy when they were young. Beattie's three daughters had seen Caroline dance when their mother had taken them to a matinee performance and they were amazed to see her dance so skilfully when she'd been such a clumsy child.

Then Lizzie and Humphrey climbed out of their car with Margaret, Isabel, Rose and Emma.

Laura looked on nervously. Caroline, who looked radiant in a cream coat and little matching cloche, was talking to Archie before entering the church. He was laughing at what she'd said, and then he patted her back affectionately.

Margaret had seen the exchange between the cousins and, white-faced, she looked at Caroline with pure hatred.

Laura glanced at Lizzie who, aware of Margaret's feelings, had taken her arm with a comforting gesture as she led her into the church. Throughout the service and at the reception afterwards Laura noticed that Lizzie was pointedly ignoring both her and Caroline.

Diana noticed the bad atmosphere between her sisters, something that had never happened among any of them since they'd grown up.

'I'll have a word with Lizzie,' she said quietly. At that moment they heard a commotion followed by a cry of shock from Caroline. Everyone turned to look at her as Margaret fled out of the room in tears. Caroline's beautiful cream coat had been splashed with hot tea, and some had dripped on to her cream suede shoes.

Laura stepped forward and calmly helped her to take off the stained garment, saying briskly, 'If it's sponged down it will be fine.'

Then she handed it to one of Beattie's maids, who looked deeply concerned. 'I'll get a damp cloth for the shoes,' she murmured, taking the coat with her.

Caroline caught her mother's eye and realized the most

dignified way to handle the situation was to pass it off as a silly accident. 'That will teach me to wear pastel-coloured clothes,' she exclaimed laughingly, although in reality she was furious. She'd done nothing to warrant Margaret's chagrin except to glow with happiness. Then she'd heard Margaret say 'Happy now?' as she threw the contents of her cup over her.

'That girl is out for blood,' Diana whispered to Laura. 'I must say I feel terribly sorry for her because she's been going out with Richard for some time and we all thought he'd marry her. When Robert and I saw them dining at the Ritz I guessed it was over for Margaret.'

Laura looked at her sister sharply. 'You didn't say you were going to the Ritz?'

Diana realized her blunder. 'At the last minute Robert insisted we spend the night at the hotel before setting off for Paris. I meant to tell you but I forgot.'

'Other people seem to know what my daughter is doing more than I do.' Laura sounded annoyed. 'It's hardly her fault if young men fall for her.'

Diana smiled. 'It's just rather unfortunate that it was Margaret's young man.'

Laura was about to snap back but Lizzie came rushing up, her face flushed and her eyes flashing angrily.

'Margaret is terribly upset,' she said breathlessly. 'She's crying her eyes out. I'll have to take her home. What did Caroline say to her? She won't tell me.'

By now Laura was also angry. 'Perhaps that's because she didn't say anything,' she retorted. 'Why are you blaming Caroline for everything?'

'Because she's a scheming little minx,' Lizzie said with frankness. 'From the moment she saw Richard Montgomery she set out to catch him.'

Laura looked at her blankly. 'I don't know what you're talking about. She's been working far too hard to chase anyone. When she comes home late at night she's utterly exhausted.'

Lizzie looked directly at her. 'I wonder why?' she asked drily as she walked away, leaving Laura looking perplexed.

Beattie came over to them at that moment in her pale blue outfit and a river of long ropes of pearls around her neck.

'This is Philip's christening,' she pointed out. 'What's going on? I've never seen you having a disagreement before. People are looking at you and apparently Margaret has left in tears.'

'It's nothing,' Diana said quietly. She looked at Laura and Lizzie. 'Perhaps we should mingle with the other guests.'

Laura felt deeply hurt that the sisters she'd always been closest to were blaming Caroline for everything. The truth was her daughter was prettier and more vivacious than Margaret, and that was not her fault. She'd also worked hard and was on the cusp of being a prima ballerina, while Margaret was just sitting and waiting for a rich young man who would make a suitable husband. A rush of maternal love for her only child threatened to overwhelm her and her eyes brimmed with tears. How dare they criticize Caroline when they all knew she'd dedicated her life to making sure her daughter had everything she wanted?

Humphrey came up to her, good, kind and dependable Humphrey. He could tell she was upset.

'I'm terribly sorry about Margaret's behaviour,' he said, taking her arm and leading her out on to the drawing-room balcony. 'I'll make sure, my dear, that Margaret writes letters of apology to both you and Caroline. What she did was utterly uncalled for and unforgiveable.'

She looked at him earnestly, grateful for his comforting remarks. 'You needn't do that, Humphrey. It's just that Lizzie and Diana act as if Caroline was to blame for breaking up Margaret and Richard's romance.'

He smiled and nodded. 'We all know what young men are like,' he said with a chuckle. 'It's better Richard chucks her now, not when they were engaged or married.'

Laura smiled, loving him for his realistic attitude. 'I have done my best to bring her up,' she began, her voice quivering.

He looked into her face. 'You've done a magnificent job, my dear. No one could have done better and you should be enormously proud of her. I'm aware of the struggle you've had what with the lack of money and being on your own, but you should be congratulated for doing a marvellous job.'

His words were like a warm, comforting balm to her battered emotions, and as he led her back into the crowded room he said, 'Now let me get you a fresh cup of tea.'

There was no sign of Caroline and Laura remembered she'd told her she'd have to slip away early from the reception because the choreographer of *Rainbows* wanted to make some changes and he'd told her she was needed for a rehearsal before the curtains went up.

Richard was waiting in his flat when Caroline arrived. 'You got away nice and early,' he said, taking her in his arms.

'Mind out, I'm soaking down my front,' she exclaimed.

He stood back and looked at her coat. 'It's slightly damp,' he corrected her. 'Did you spill something?'

'No, Margaret threw a cup of boiling hot tea over me. It could have scalded me.' She took off her coat and threw it on a chair. 'It ruined my afternoon.'

Richard backed away, looking worried. 'Is she all right?'

Caroline stared at him. 'What do you mean? She could have burned my legs and I'm on stage in two-and-a-half hours. She's ruined my day. She could have scalded my feet. Don't you understand?'

'If she really attacked you in front of everyone she must be upset about you and I being together.'

Caroline shrugged. 'It's not my fault, though.'

He held her close. 'No, it's my fault. It's you I love and you I want, my darling.' Kissing her passionately, he started to undo the little buttons down the back of her silk dress.

Walter sounded anxious when he telephoned Laura the following week. 'Rowena really is unwell,' he explained. 'The doctor has been again and he's prescribed something stronger to ease the pain just under her ribs,' he explained.

'I'm sorry to hear that,' Laura replied. 'It sounds like a stomach ulcer.'

'I think it's more serious than that. She's lost a lot of weight and she's so weak she can hardly get out of bed.'

'Perhaps she should be admitted to hospital.'

'You know what she's like. Stubborn as a mule,' he replied.

Laura and Rowena had never been friends, and when Walter's first wife had died she'd wanted him to come and live with her because, having been widowed and without children, she was desperately lonely. Nevertheless, Laura was grateful that thanks to Rowena and a wonderful doctor, Walter hadn't touched alcohol for nearly fifteen years.

'Is there anything I can do?' Laura asked. 'I can't leave Caroline alone in London. Beattie has her hands full with the new baby and I fear Lizzie will never speak to Caroline again.' Then she told him about the tea-throwing incident.

Walter chuckled. 'I'm surprised Caroline didn't chuck a very large jug of water over Margaret's head in retaliation.'

'In fact, Caroline behaved beautifully. You'd have been proud of her.'

'I always am,' he said quietly. 'How much longer is *Rainbows* on for? Perhaps you can both come and stay for a few days.' There was a note of longing in his voice.

'Of course,' Laura agreed stoutly, 'and I hope Rowena is better soon.'

She noticed Walter didn't reply. He just said, 'Goodbye, my dear.'

'I wish I could stay all night with you,' Caroline sighed as she slid out of Richard's bed. It was Sunday and she'd told her mother she was spending the day with Violet, one of the dancers whose birthday it was.

'I think her parents are giving a big luncheon party,' she'd added vaguely. She had told her mother so many lies in the past few weeks that she had to be careful not to get caught out. If only Richard would propose then she wouldn't have to lie at all.

'Where would you like to have luncheon?' he asked.

'Nowhere smart,' she said quickly. 'I can't risk being recognized. We were seen at the Ritz and at the Savoy. My mother will kill me if she finds out I'm seeing you.'

Richard smiled. 'Why don't we drive to the country and have lunch in a pub?'

It flashed through her mind that Aunt Georgie and Uncle Shane owned several pubs. Supposing they went to one of theirs? 'I don't think so,' she said firmly. 'I'd like to go to a small restaurant in London, but not in Kensington or Belgravia.'

Richard burst out laughing. 'Why are you so afraid of being seen with me? Am I that dreadful?'

There was silence and Caroline's face reddened. 'My mother doesn't know I'm seeing you.'

Richard looked disappointed. 'You mean she doesn't even know we're just seeing each other innocently? I never went to bed with Margaret, you know.'

Caroline's dark eyes widened. 'Why not?' she asked bluntly.

Richard shrugged. 'I suppose I wasn't in love with her in the way I'm in love with you.'

She grabbed her clothes and started to get dressed again. 'You mean she wasn't that sort of girl?' Her voice was shrill with anger. 'It shows you respected her but you've no respect for me!'

'Hey! Where did all this come from?' He looked dumbfounded.

'My mother was right! Oh, God! I wish I'd never met you. Now you'll tell your friends I'm an "easy girl". Isn't that what they're called?' She was crying now and her face was blotchy.

'Listen to me, Caroline, and stop being ridiculous.' His voice was commanding. 'I love you and respect you from the bottom of my heart. I told you I didn't sleep with Margaret because I thought you'd be pleased. It means you are the one I truly love and I want to be with.'

She'd quietened down but she gave a little sob, reminding him of a child. 'Come here,' he said, going towards her with open arms.

'I was afraid . . .' she began.

'I know, my darling. You need never be afraid again. I'll always be here for you.' He was holding her close, his cheek pressed against her cheek.

'You promise?' she whispered.

'I promise.'

Thirteen

'Is that you, Dada?'

Walter recognized her voice on the telephone and she sounded excited.

'Hello, my darling. How are you?' he asked.

'Wonderfully well,' Caroline replied enthusiastically. 'Something wonderful has happened. You know *Rainbows* closed in March? Well, I went to an audition last week and guess what?'

He chuckled. 'You got yourself another job?'

'Not just a job, Dada. I got the leading role of principle ballerina in *The Fairy Queen*. It's being produced at Drury Lane which is the most famous theatre in London and I'm going to be the Fairy Queen!'

'Well done, sweetheart! That's marvellous news. Your mother must be pleased. After all her hard work to send you to ballet school she must be very proud of you,' he said warmly.

'It's me who has done the hard work,' Caroline protested crossly. 'Some nights my toenails are bleeding! You will come to the first night, won't you?'

There was a pause before he answered. 'I may not be able to,' he said carefully.

'Why not?' she demanded.

'Your Aunt Rowena isn't at all well. In fact, I'm very worried about her.'

'But you can't miss my first appearance at Drury Lane! To be performing at Drury Lane! Aunt Rowena has got servants, hasn't she? Why should you miss my performance because of her?'

Walter's mouth tightened. 'Because she's looked after me for years, and because she needs me to support her, which I'm more than willing to do. Caroline, you are not the only pebble on the beach, you know,' he added firmly.

'But Dada . . .'

'There are no "buts" where human kindness comes first. You're letting success go to your head, my dear.'

He heard a click and then silence. Caroline had hung up. Sighing, he felt a deep sense of disappointment. His daughter was showing all the signs of a spoilt brat. She'd been such a lovely little girl and she could still be charming, but only if she got her own way.

Tapping on his sister's bedroom door a few minutes later, he heard her say, 'Come in' in a frail voice. The local doctor had arranged for a nurse to come to the house every morning to give her a blanket bath and make sure she was comfortable for the day.

Rowena was sitting up in bed, ashen-faced and gaunt.

'That was Caroline on the telephone,' he said, doing his best to sound cheerful. 'She's got another job and they've given her the leading role.'

'That's good. You must go down to London to see her.' Even though suffering great pain, Rowena struggled to be polite.

'I'm not going anywhere until you're better.'

She gave a wan smile. 'That's never going to happen, and you know it.'

The silence in the room was oppressive. Then he spoke. 'If that's the case I won't be going anywhere. You've supported me for God knows how long and I'm going to support you now.'

She reached for his hand. 'Thank you. You've always been a good brother to me.'

Cranley Court, 1923

'I've been thinking.' Diana announced as she and Robert sat down to luncheon in their formal and elegant dining room.

'Steady on, old girl,' he teased.

Diana laughed. 'Seriously, I think we should rent a big house in London, just for the season. We're missing a lot of fun by staying here all the time, lovely though it is.'

'May I ask why you think London is such fun?' he inquired.

'As we've only got one daughter I think Emily should become a debutante and do the season properly. Lizzie tells me she's bringing out Isabel in a big way so Margaret has another shot at finding a husband. Beattie and Andrew are very sociable too. They're always having interesting people to dinner and I feel like a country bumpkin beside them.'

Robert looked out of the window at the manicured lawns surrounding Crawley Manor and forest and the mountains beyond. It was obvious he loved the beauty of the Scottish countryside.

'Did your mother bring out all eight of you and your sisters?' he asked.

'Yes, but then we had Lochlee Castle and she entertained all year round. High society came up to us. We didn't go to London to meet everyone.'

'I remember,' Robert said with a grin. 'I stayed for a shoot and fell in love with you.'

Diana smiled, remembering how well Robert had danced the reels and how handsome he'd been in his kilt and a sapphire-blue velvet doublet. How young they'd been in those days and how innocent she'd been! She'd even had to go to Lizzie, who was already married, to ask what actually happened on her wedding night.

'Now that Queen Victoria is dead I believe the parties at Buckingham Palace are good fun for the first time in fifty years,' she added laughingly. 'Do let's go to London, just for May, June and July. That will give us plenty of time to get ready for the twelfth of August.'

Robert looked thoughtful. 'I'll agree on one condition.'

'What's that?' she asked cautiously.

He leaned forward so no one would hear him. 'The condition is I can take you to Paris again for another naughty weekend.'

'Oh, yes, please,' she responded with a knowing smile.

London, 1923

'I'll be away for the weekend,' Caroline announced casually as she and Laura had breakfast. 'Sally has invited me to stay with

her and her parents on Saturday at their home in Sussex and
I'll be back on Sunday afternoon. You don't mind, do you?'
she added with unusual politeness.

'Do I know Sally? Where do they live in Sussex?' Laura
asked. Caroline was always trotting out the names of different
girls and she seemed suddenly to have acquired a lot of girlfriends since they'd come to London. She hated feeling as if
she didn't entirely trust her daughter but what was she to do?
There had been no mention of Richard Montgomery for weeks
now but that didn't mean anything. The last time she'd asked
about him Caroline had exploded with anger and accused her
of being a jailor.

'Sally is another dancer and her parents live near a place
called Hazelmere.'

'Why don't you invite some of your friends here? We could
do a buffet supper one evening before you start rehearsing for
The Fairy Queen. Wouldn't that be a good idea, and pay back
some of the hospitality you've received.'

'It's a ghastly idea. This flat is far too small for a party. I
must go or I'll be late.' A moment later the front door crashed
shut.

For the first time in her life, Laura felt helpless. Caroline
was a grown woman, wilful and selfish, who didn't care
about anybody but herself. Over and over again she wondered
if she'd been too lenient a mother? Or had she been too
strict? Was that why Caroline was rebelling now? Normally
she'd have talked to Lizzie, who with four daughters had a
lot of experience, but Lizzie was chilly towards her these
days.

Sitting in her lovely drawing room, Laura felt more alone
than she'd ever done. Beattie was busy with little Philip and
Diana was far away in Scotland, as were Alice and Flora.
Georgie now had five children and from what Laura could
gather she had no control over any of them. In the past she'd
enjoyed it when her clients came for fittings or to choose
designs and fabric with her. Now she couldn't help feeling
very lonely.

At that moment the telephone rang. Glad for the distraction,
she went into the hall to answer it.

'Laura? It's Walter.' He sounded very down and she immediately asked if he was all right.

'I've been better,' he admitted. 'I'm phoning to tell you that
Rowena died a little while ago. I was with her and she just
faded peacefully away.'

'I'm terribly sorry to hear that,' she replied with concern.
'You must be heartbroken. Are you all right, Walter?'

'Yes. I've been expecting it for some time but it's always a
shock when it happens.'

'What are you going to do now?'

'I've been making a lot of plans, Laura. I can't talk now but
I'll get in touch again in a few days' time.'

'I'll come to her funeral, if you'd like that.'

'There's no need. She told me she didn't want any fuss and
said she wanted to be cremated.'

'But who is going to look after you?' she asked anxiously.

'I can look after myself,' he retorted. 'Don't worry. I'm not
about to seek solace in drink ever again. I'm not a child and
nor am I infirm,' he added almost impatiently.

She'd forgotten what a proud man he'd been in his youth.

'I know that but if you need anything just let me know,'
Laura replied.

After they'd said goodbye she worried that in spite of his
protestations he'd turn to drink once again. The sensible side
of her nature told her he was no longer her problem but her
emotions told her that at some point he'd need the companionship of someone close to him, but who now that his sister
was dead?

What had he meant when he said he'd been making a lot
of plans? And why didn't he want her to accompany him to
Rowena's funeral? At that moment she was struck by a possi-
bility that to her surprise made her extremely jealous.

Richard kissed her neck with tenderness as they lay on the
bed after making love. 'You're so beautiful,' he whispered,
stroking her shoulder. Caroline looked up at him, her dark
eyes filled with adoration. He was everything to her in every
way. Nothing could spoil her happiness now, she told herself
as she lay in his arms.

After a while they rose to get dressed and he said casually, 'I wish I wasn't being sent to New York.'

'New York in America?' she asked stupidly.

'It was in the USA the last time I worked there,' he replied flippantly as he tied the laces of his polished black shoes.

Caroline felt sick with dismay, her lovely world of having someone in her life who loved her and looked after her by taking her to expensive restaurants slowly crumbling.

'Why?' she asked as tears welled up in her eyes.

'I meant to tell you,' he said, blushing crimson. 'The company I work for wants me to set up an office in Wall Street and I'll only be away for three months while you'll be busy entertaining ecstatic audiences at Drury Lane.'

'Three months,' she repeated, turning pale. 'You're dumping me, aren't you? This is your way of doing it because you haven't the courage to tell me to my face that you're bored with me.' She was hysterical now and the tears were pouring down her cheeks. 'You bastard!' she shrieked. 'You're dumping me like you dumped Margaret.'

Caroline sat down on the bed.

Richard turned on her angrily. 'What on earth are you talking about? Of course I love you and I don't want to be away for three months. This is the work that I do, like the work you do as a dancer. I bet you'll have to tour all over Britain with *The Fairy Queen* and I'll miss you dreadfully but I'd never accuse you of trying to dump me. You must believe that, darling.'

Caroline sank back on the bed, exhausted by her outburst.

Richard sat down beside her, looking concerned. 'I'll write to you every week, although compared to you my news won't be very exciting,' he assured her. 'I'll be stuck in an office from dawn to dusk and all the time I'll be missing you.'

'If you really loved me you'd refuse to go,' she pointed out.

'Now you are being silly. I have a job to do and so do you. If I do well it will lead to promotion and I'll be earning a lot more when I return. I'm thinking of buying a house in Knightsbridge.'

'That would be nice,' she remarked, brightening.

'You can help me do it up.'

'When do you go?'

'In two days' time.'

'So soon?' she exclaimed.

'The sooner I go the sooner I'll be back,' he said cheerfully. 'You've got your mother and a big family to support you on your first night.'

'I told you she doesn't know I've been seeing you,' Caroline said in a small voice.

Richard looked at her in astonishment. 'Still? Then who does she think you are spending so much time with?'

'Just friends from the ballet world. Aunt Lizzie blames me for stealing you away from Margaret. My mother is very protective and she's terrified I'll get into trouble, so it's easier to let her think I've got lots of girlfriends.'

He looked perturbed. 'So you've been lying to her?'

Caroline shrugged. 'It was easier. She's very strict.'

He rose and looked down at her. 'We have no future if you're frightened to tell her we have been seeing each other,' he pointed out.

'All right. I'll tell her but she'll be terribly angry that I've lied to her. I think I'll wait until you return and we can tell her together.'

Richard looked surprised and rather disconcerted. 'As you wish,' he replied coolly.

'Did you know that Richard has gone to America?' Lizzie asked Margaret as they sat in the morning room going through first the letters that had been delivered and also the Court Circular of *The Times* and the *Telegraph* to see who had been 'Hatched, Matched and Dispatched'.

'So he's dumped Caroline too, has he?' her daughter asked, her face lighting up at the news.

'I don't know,' Lizzie replied, 'but I suppose he must have. I believe he's gone for several months.'

'How did you find out?'

'I saw his mother at a luncheon party and she told me. We were great friends until recently and I think she feels rather guilty that he led you up the garden path.'

Margaret sighed. 'Lady Montgomery would have been a lovely mother-in-law.'

'She was very fond of you, too. She was also talking to another friend about the season. There are going to be balls almost every night and I'll make sure you get asked to most of them. Aunt Diana is going to bring out Emily and we've decided to give a joint coming-out ball for Isabel and Emily. That will be fun, won't it?'

Margaret perked up. 'It's a great idea, and I can get to know a few more young men,' she replied with alacrity.

Lizzie looked delighted. 'That's settled then. We must start making plans. I have a feeling it's going to be a very good season.'

Rehearsals for *The Fairy Queen* started at ten o'clock in the morning and sometimes lasted the whole day.

Depressed and missing Richard, Caroline felt drained of energy and at times so tired she wanted to curl up in a quiet corner and sleep. Back again at the same rehearsal rooms at Baron's Court, she realized that even her enthusiasm for ballet had waned in spite of the fact she was the prima ballerina. She'd struggled for years to reach this position so why was she reluctant to get out of bed in the morning? A few days later she was sick after her mother had made her scrambled eggs for breakfast.

Laura turned pale as Caroline came stumbling out of the bathroom.

'You're pregnant, aren't you?' she asked in a shocked voice.

'Of course I'm not,' Caroline snapped, but Laura saw the terror in her dark eyes.

'My God, you are pregnant.' Laura was filled with anguish. 'You've slept with that young man, haven't you? You stupid, stupid girl! This will ruin your career! How can you perform when you're pregnant? How did you think you could hide your pregnancy, for God's sake?' Laura was so shocked and disappointed she couldn't even think straight.

'But I'm not pregnant!' Caroline protested. 'I can't be.'

'I watched my mother being pregnant and each time she looked just like you do; tired, listless and sick in the morning. How could you let this happen? I've told you over and over again that you mustn't sleep with a man until you were married to him.'

'I can have an abortion. I know several girls who had abortions.' Then she grabbed her coat and handbag and a moment later she was gone.

The shock left Laura feeling both unwell and sick. Neither she nor any of her sisters had slept with their future husbands until their wedding night. Their mother had made it very clear that to do so was wrong. Things may be changing and surely it was the man's responsibility to take precautions. Her greatest fear at the moment was that the rest of the family would look upon Caroline as a slut in future. She recalled when they all lived in Lochlee Castle a housemaid had become pregnant by one of the footmen and it led to the poor girl being put in a terrible institution for unmarried mothers by her family. As for having an abortion, that was murder and an even worse sin. There was only one solution: Richard Montgomery had to return to England and marry Caroline. She would write to Sir George Montgomery immediately and demand that his son return to England and make an honest woman of her daughter.

'My dear Laura,' Walter said with concern when she telephoned him to tell him what had happened. 'Do you know this young man? Would he be a suitable husband for Caroline?'

'If he was good enough for Margaret he's good enough for Caroline. I'm going mad with worry and she didn't come home last night,' Laura added.

There was a pause before Walter said, 'Are you sure it's his baby she's expecting? Is there another man in her life?'

'Don't! Don't!' Laura burst into tears. 'I brought her up so carefully and now I feel I've let her down. How could she let this happen when she knew how terrible the consequences could be? Even if Richard marries her quickly it will get out that he was forced into it. I wish now we'd never come to London.'

'In life one has to take the rough with the smooth, my dear. I'm rather tied up with things at the moment but let me know what's happening, won't you?'

When he'd hung up, Laura had never felt so alone in her life. What did he mean by being 'tied up with things at the moment'? His sister was dead and his son by his first marriage

was living with his grandparents and working for a big firm
of accountants. Then Laura was struck by a shattering thought
which sent her brain spinning. Had Walter got a new woman
in his life? He'd always been attractive to women and Rowena
had always made sure none of them got close to him because
without his companionship she'd have been terribly lonely in
Dalkeith.

A pang of jealousy surged through Laura's heart, taking her
by surprise. They'd been separated for years and now, perhaps
too late, she realized how much she loved him.

Fourteen

New York, 1923

Richard read and re-read his father's cable for the umpteenth time as he tried to take in what the future held for him. He was in love with Caroline but he'd been in love several times. Then he'd meet someone new and fall in love all over again. For one thing he didn't feel ready to settle down at twenty-six. As for starting a family, the very thought of it filled him with horror. He'd been so careful too. Unfortunately there was no way he could deny it was his baby, much as he longed to. Caroline had been a virgin when they met and he knew he was the only man in her life.

Sighing deeply, he rose from his desk, walked over to the large window and gazed at the magnificent skyscrapers of Manhattan with sad eyes. His office was on the twenty-third floor and never before had he seen such a modern spectacle. He wanted to stay here for ever. London suddenly struck him as being old fashioned but how could he remain here when Caroline's future was in Europe?

New York was a magical city teeming with energy, where anything seemed possible. The thought of returning to England to get married and await the birth of his child now seemed like a prison sentence – a neat little cell from which there was no hope of escape. In the cable his father sounded more sad than angry and that was the only solace Richard had to hang on to. His parents were full of regret rather than anger. He'd messed up his life and possibly his career if he couldn't return to New York immediately after his wedding, but he had to do the honourable thing and he had to do it with grace and a show of enthusiasm. He was trapped in a ghastly situation of his own making and that was indeed the bitterest pill to swallow.

★ ★ ★

The voice on the telephone was unfamiliar. 'Could I speak to Lady Laura Leighton-Harvey, please?' a woman asked politely.

'It's me speaking,' Laura replied.

'This is Lady Montgomery, Richard's mother,' she announced in a friendly manner. 'You must be cursing the day my son was born and wishing your daughter had never met him, and who could blame you?' she prattled on sympathetically.

'It is a blow,' Laura admitted. 'Have you been in touch with your son?'

'We have indeed and he's booked his passage on the next ship to England, so he'll be back in seven or eight days. He's asked his father to arrange for them to marry by special license in a registry office and I wondered if you'd like to come to luncheon so we can discuss the arrangements?'

Laura felt like crying that Caroline was to be robbed of a beautiful white wedding in a church, surrounded by all the family, with Walter to give her away.

'Under the circumstances I don't think there are many arrangements to make, do you?' Laura replied as she struggled to control her emotions.

'I can understand how you feel,' Honor Montgomery replied, 'but I can assure you Richard is mad about Caroline. He told me he can't wait to marry her and I know he'll look after her. Now, when can you come to luncheon? The sooner the better as far as George and I are concerned.'

So that would be that. Mission accomplished, thought Laura as she gripped the phone tightly with a trembling hand. A contract signed, sealed and delivered with about as much warmth as completing the contract for her flat.

'How about the day after tomorrow?' Honour suggested.

'Yes, that would be fine,' Laura said evenly.

'Splendid! Shall we say one o'clock? We're in Green Street. Number thirty-two. We're so looking forward to meeting you,' gushed Honor. 'See you then. Goodbye.'

When Laura put down the telephone she realized Honor Montgomery hadn't shown any eagerness to meet Caroline.

Laura immediately telephoned Walter. It was a shock when the housekeeper at Dalkeith House announced that Mr Leighton-

Harvey was away for a couple of days and could she take a message?

A sense of panic swept through Laura. 'Do you know where he's staying?'

'I'm afraid not, Lady Laura, but if he contacts me shall I ask him to get in touch with you?'

'Yes, please, and tell him it's urgent.'

When Caroline returned from rehearsals Laura told her everything that Richard's mother had said.

'So Richard is coming back? What about his job? Will he have to return to America again? Oh, I do hope so. Then he and I can get a place of our own. I hate this flat.'

It felt to Laura as though another bit of her heart had broken. 'I thought you liked it here. Anyway, I'll find out tomorrow what Richard's plans are,' Laura added.

'She's nice to your face but she's probably telling all her friends that I'm a complete trollop and worse still I'm on the stage and that automatically means I'm a low-life in their eyes. When is Dada coming to London?'

'I'm not sure. He seems to be very busy,' Laura added, a touch crisply.

'I expect he's busy sorting out Aunt Rowena's stuff but I do miss him. It was so nice when he stayed with us.' She sounded wistful, her face crumbling, then she burst into tears and flung her arms around her mother.

'I'm so sorry, Muzzie. I'm always being horrid to you and you've always been wonderful to me and given me everything,' she sobbed. 'And I've disappointed you now, haven't I? I know I'm bringing disgrace on the family and I'm so sorry.'

Laura held her only child who she loved more than life itself close while a distraught Caroline clung on to her like a little girl. Laura was remembering how happy she'd been when Caroline was born. From that moment on everything she'd done, every decision she'd made had been whatever was best for Caroline. Maybe she should have stayed with Walter instead of letting his sister care for him, but she'd done what she'd done to make a living so that her daughter's dreams of being the next Anna Pavlova could come true.

'I love you so much, darling,' she said softly, 'and we will get through this. Your career needn't suffer and I can help you when the baby arrives.'

Caroline looked straight into her mother's eyes. 'I love you too, Muzzie. I really do, and I'm sorry I lied to you when I was actually seeing Richard. Thank God he wants to marry me, and anyway, you'll be the best granny ever.'

The house in Green Street was large and imposing, and as Laura rang the brass bell she realized that at least the Montgomeries were wealthy, so Caroline wasn't marrying a pauper. She should have guessed that Lizzie had hoped Margaret was going to marry a rich man as well as an aristocrat.

Sir George and Lady Montgomery were waiting for her in their comfortable but grand drawing room on the first floor of the six-story house. Honor came forward immediately and clasped Laura's hand.

'Lady Laura, thank you so much for coming. I'm most terribly sorry Richard has caused this crisis. He says he really loves your daughter and he told me to tell you that he was planning to propose when he returned to England.'

Laura, tall and elegant in a navy blue dress and jacket and a matching hat with a large brim, smiled politely, not sure whether Honor Montgomery was sincere or not.

'It is a bit of a disaster,' she replied, 'and Caroline is very shocked that she allowed this to happen.'

Sir George strode across the room to shake her hand. 'If my son was younger I'd have horsewhipped him,' he said in jovial tones. 'I don't know what's the matter with young people these days. My father would probably have shot me if I'd got Honor pregnant before we were married. Now, can I offer you a glass of sherry before we have luncheon?'

'Thank you.' Sitting down on the sofa beside Honor, Laura realized they talked the same language, held the same views and were perfect future in-laws for Caroline.

'I gather your daughter is a ballet dancer?' Sir George said at that moment in rather scathing terms, which made Laura have second thoughts about their suitability. 'I imagine she'll give it up right away,' he continued briskly.

'Absolutely not,' Laura retorted forcefully. 'She's the prima ballerina in *The Fairy Queen* which opens in a few days. It would be a terrible waste of her talent and Madame Espinosa who spent years training her would agree.'

There was a stony silence broken by Honor saying, 'A little more sherry, Lady Laura?'

'No, thank you,' said Laura with a polite smile, feeling she had won the first round.

'Do you want the marriage kept a secret for the time being?' Sir George asked.

'Not at all. Surely the more people who know the better? Of course, they're going to realize what's happened, but at least they will have been married for seven months before the baby is born.'

Sir George looked annoyed. 'You do know that as soon as they're married Richard has to go back to New York for a couple of months or maybe even longer? Wouldn't it look better if Caroline returned to New York with Richard and they could get a lovely apartment and live there for a couple of years? None of us need to mention the baby until it's quite big and no one need know your daughter is already pregnant. I'm suggesting this to spare your daughter's reputation.'

Laura felt quite sick. Things were moving so fast, life-altering plans were being suggested and she felt she was losing control of the situation; something she swore would never happen again when the bailiffs arrived without warning to strip her of her home and all her possessions. If there was one thing that rattled her it was losing control of what was happening in her life. The thought of not being close to Caroline as her pregnancy progressed and not being around to help with the baby was like a knife through her heart.

'Caroline is desperately keen to dance this leading role, and if she's well enough to do it then I think she should,' Laura said firmly.

There was another silence and Laura began to wonder if they wanted Richard to marry Caroline at all.

Honor rose from the sofa. 'Let's go down to luncheon,' she announced. 'How is your sister, Lizzie? I haven't seen her for a while?'

'She's not very happy that your son prefers Caroline to her daughter Margaret.'

Honor gave a tinkling laugh. 'Oh dear! Yes, he was in love with Margaret and quite a few other girls before her.'

'Really?' Laura said drily.

'Where are you planning to hold the wedding reception?' Sir George swiftly enquired as they trooped down the stairs to the dining room. 'Claridges is excellent for that sort of thing.'

'I haven't made any plans yet but my sister Beattie has a big house in Belgravia. I think I might ask her if we can hold it there. Hotels are so impersonal, aren't they?'

Later that day, Laura telephoned Walter wanting to tell him about Richard's parents, only to be told by one of the servants that he was out.

'Will you tell him that his wife called and can he ring me back when he gets in?' she asked.

'He said he might be quite late, ma'am.'

Laura was becoming seriously anxious. What on earth was he up to? Of one thing she was sure: he wasn't drinking again. He'd told her he couldn't even bear the smell of liquor. So what was keeping him so 'busy' since Rowena's death?

It could only be one thing: he'd met another woman. A burning feeling of jealousy surged through her, leaving her in a panic. What a fool she'd been to turn him away when they'd gone bankrupt.

Sitting alone in her flat as it grew dark outside, she wondered what sort of woman had attracted him. A tall and slender version of herself? Much younger than she was and more beautiful? A war widow perhaps and very comfortably off, perhaps. Tears slid down her cheeks. What a mess she'd made of her life and what a mess Caroline was making of her life, she reflected.

The room was in darkness now and she was startled when the telephone in the hall rang. Stumbling out of the drawing room, she cleared her throat so the caller wouldn't know she was crying.

'Is that you, Laura?' Walter sounded mystified. 'Are you all right, my dear? I'm sorry I was out when you called. How is everything going? You sound very down.'

'I had luncheon with the Montgomeries today.' She proceeded to tell him what they'd suggested about Caroline and Richard living in New York for several years so that no one in this country would know exactly when the baby was born.

'That's a rotten notion,' Walter exclaimed. 'The truth always comes out sooner or later. Look, I'm very tied up at the moment but I'll come down to see you and Caroline next week. I'll book into a nearby hotel. I need to talk to you, Laura.'

Her heart seemed to stumble. 'What about?'

'The future,' he said hurriedly. 'I must go, my dear – someone has just arrived to see me.'

She heard him say to the maid in muffled voice, 'Please show Mrs Hamilton into the drawing room.'

Then he spoke into the telephone again. 'Sorry about that, Laura. Give my love to Caroline. Goodbye for now.' There was a click and silence, which left Laura wondering who Mrs Hamilton was.

Stunned, she bid him goodbye. Walter was acting out of character and this time it wasn't the drink. She had a terrible feeling that it wasn't Caroline's future he wanted to discuss but their own divorce because he wanted to marry someone else – someone called 'Mrs Hamilton'.

Caroline was torn between feelings of anxiety that she wouldn't be able to dance as well as she normally did and that the choreographer would decide she wasn't good enough to dance at all. Her stomach was still flat but she bought a boned corset with lacing at the back which could be pulled tighter and tighter so her pregnancy wouldn't show. Richard would be back in New York by the time she started bulging so she'd have to find someone else to help her, but who? Muzzie would disapprove but who else could she trust? All she wanted was to get rave reviews, her picture in the newspapers and her contract extended. She longed for them to say she was better than Anna Pavlova. The desire to be a better ballerina energized her. Nothing was going to stop her succeeding. Not a baby. Not marriage. Absolutely nothing now would stop her from getting to the top of her profession.

Her fears lay in her family's disapproval. Aunt Lizzie was already angry over her romance with Richard; now she was pregnant it would be a family disgrace. She also feared they'd think she was a terrible example to her female cousins. Would she for ever be the only member of the Fairbairn family to be saved 'from ending up in the gutter' by her mother writing to Richard's parents and demanding he should make a respectable woman of her? How could it be so wrong to make love? Why would everyone look down on her if they knew? She'd become the black sheep of the family and Muzzie was bearing the brunt, she reflected, wishing she'd been kinder to her in the past. She wasn't even sure why she felt so angry most of the time towards her mother, who had given her life to see she had everything she wanted. Or was it jealousy of all her rich cousins? She hoped she'd make a good mother when the baby arrived but what was she going to do with it? Perhaps Richard could afford for them to have a nanny. Then, before she could stop herself, she thought she could always give it to Muzzie to look after.

Laura was pleasantly surprised when Beattie arrived to see her the following day.

'How lovely to see you. How is little Philip?' she asked, leading the way into her drawing room.

'He's wonderful and such a good baby. They always say boys are much easier than girls,' Beattie replied laughingly.

'You'll stay and have a cup of tea, won't you?'

'I'd love that and I'm sorry to turn up like this, but I've been to a luncheon party where I heard an astonishing bit of gossip. I just had to come and see you to find out if it's true.'

Laura's heart sank as she guessed what was coming. 'Who were you lunching with?'

'Priscilla Cavendish. She and her husband live in Grosvenor Square and she invited ten of her girlfriends to have luncheon. I knew most of them, which was fun.'

'Was Honor Montgomery one of her guests?' Laura asked with a distressed expression.

Beattie shook her head. 'No, she wasn't, but her name was mentioned. Apparently she'd told Emma Fortiscue that Richard's girlfriend was pregnant and what a shame it was because he doesn't feel ready for marriage but now he has no choice . . .' Her voice faltered as she saw Laura turn pale. 'Oh my God, so it is true? Caroline's name wasn't mentioned so I presumed he'd got himself a new girlfriend. What a bastard! What's happening? Oh, Laura, what a shock for you, too.'

Laura covered her face with both hands. 'Yes, it's a nightmare but Richard is going to marry her by special licence in a few days' time. I'd stupidly hoped we could keep it a secret but thanks to Honor Montgomery it's going to be the talk of the town,' she added bitterly.

'What about her solo in *The Fairy Queen?*'

'She's feeling all right so far and luckily it's a secret from the ballet world, but I don't know if it will remain a secret for much longer.'

'Why didn't you tell me what was happening? Do all the others know?' Beattie asked indignantly.

'Walter is the only person who knows and I hope he'll come down to London in a few days.'

'So Lizzie doesn't know?'

'No one in the family knows. I've met Richard's parents and it's going to be a Caxton Hall affair. I was going to ask you if I could give a small reception in your house? The Montgomeries suggested Claridges but it would be terribly expensive and I'm not made of money.'

'Of course you can, dearest. What a shock this must have been for you. How is Caroline taking it?'

'She's determined to continue her career no matter what. I don't know whether she's looking forward to the actual wedding. It's not going to be the big white wedding which both she and I had dreamed of her having one day, but that's life, isn't it? Nothing works out the way we planned.'

Beattie looked thoughtful. 'That's quite sad, isn't it? When are you going to tell the others? Gossip travels like a forest fire and you don't want them hearing what's happened from anyone else.'

'I know,' Laura groaned. 'I can't put off the inevitable any longer. I'd better call on Lizzie right away. Oh, God! This is going to be difficult.'

'I'll come with you. Let's go now,' Beattie said, rising to her feet. 'The car is waiting outside and we can be there in ten minutes. You never know, maybe Lizzie will be so relieved that it's Caroline he made pregnant and not Margaret.'

Laura put on her hat and a very smart coat with red fox fur cuffs. Then she picked up her gloves and handbag. 'At least I don't have to face Mama,' she announced pragmatically. 'She'd have been really shocked at a granddaughter who got pregnant out of wedlock. When you think of it, Mama had nine daughters, six of whom have married and we were all virgins on our wedding night.'

Beattie giggled and looked at her askance. 'Speak for yourself, my dear!' she said in a low voice.

'You mean . . .?' Laura looked stunned.

Beattie nodded. 'Andrew was very persuasive.'

'Weren't you nervous?'

Her sister laughed out loud. 'I was petrified. Now I have three daughters to watch, although I don't know how on earth one stops a runaway train.'

Lizzie was at home listening to dance music on a new His Master's Voice wind-up gramophone that Humphrey had bought.

'Come in, girls,' she shouted as the butler announced them. Lizzie continued excitedly, 'I've been to this wonderful shop called Woolworths where you can get the latest gramophone records for sixpence. I want to choose the best tunes for Isabel's coming-out ball.' She seized her notepad and pencil. 'I'm making a list to give to the band that night. Isn't this one romantic? It's called "I Cover the Waterfront in Search of My Dreams".'

'Isn't that rather a long title?' Beattie queried.

'It's the first line,' Lizzie replied unabashed. There's also "Let's Make Hay While the Sun is Shining"! Isn't that a jolly tune?' She was whirling around the drawing room with an imaginary partner.

Laura caught Beattie's eye and nodded in agreement.

'Some of us have been doing just that.' Beattie had to shout to be heard over the music.

'I have something to tell you,' Laura added loudly.

'Wait a minute, I'll make the music quieter,' said Lizzie, rushing over to the gramophone where she stuffed a pair of Humphrey's woollen shooting socks down a hole in the machine. Instantly the sound faded and became gentle background music.

'Come and sit down, girls. So what have you come to tell me?' Lizzie asked.

The music had jarred Laura's nerves and she wasn't in the mood for light banter.

'That bloody man we met here has made Caroline pregnant . . .' Laura snapped. 'They're getting married at Caxton Hall and Beattie is very kindly letting me give a family reception in her house.' Then Laura sank into an armchair, overcome with emotion.

Lizzie and Beattie looked at each other in silent shock, both hoping this calamity would never happen to their daughters.

Then Laura spoke. 'I'm so sorry, Lizzie. It's supposed to be a secret and I'm going out of my mind with worry. I wish she'd never met Richard.'

Lizzie rushed over to where Laura was sitting and put her arm around her shoulder. 'If he's the sort of man who let's this happen I wish Margaret had never met him either.'

'That's what I said when I heard,' Beattie pointed out. 'At least he's going to marry her.'

Laura felt very relieved that Lizzie and she were close once more and decided to unburden herself completely. This was the moment to be grateful to be part of a large family.

'I'm worried about Walter, too,' Laura admitted when they'd finishing talking about Caroline's future.

They looked sharply at her. 'He hasn't gone back to drinking, has he?' Beattie asked.

'No. I think he's got a lady friend and I'm terribly afraid he's going to ask for a divorce. He said he had things to do and while we were talking someone arrived and he told the maid to show a Mrs Hamilton into the drawing room.'

'He's probably lonely without his sister and this woman is just a friend,' Lizzie remarked in practical tones.

Laura shook her head. 'He's up to something. I can tell because he's become rather evasive, which isn't like him. He's also booked himself into a hotel instead of staying with us when he comes to London.'

Beattie and Lizzie exchanged knowing looks and Laura rose to leave.

'I must get home now – Caroline will be back from rehearsing.'

Beattie got to her feet. 'I'll give you a lift, dearest, and try not to worry.'

Laura gave a wan smile. People had been telling her that all her life and it really didn't help at all.

Caroline stared at the words in the telegram she'd been sent. Cold, unfeeling words that made her heart sink with dread.

Meet me at my flat on Sunday, 3 p.m. Richard.

Not even a hint of friendliness, far less affection.

'When is he coming back?' Laura asked. At that moment she couldn't even bring herself to name the man who had caused such a calamity.

Caroline dropped into a chair. 'Tomorrow,' she replied in a flat voice. 'I'd imagined he'd come here to see me.' She handed the telegram to her mother. 'It's very curt. He's probably furious that I'm expecting a baby but it's his fault, too. At least he will be here for the first night on Tuesday. I want him to see what I have to sacrifice for this child.'

'Be sure not to put all the blame on him,' Laura advised gently.

'I don't know what I'd do without you, Muzzie. That cable has made me wonder if he even cares for me? Now I don't know if he even likes me any more. I'm terrified he'll walk away before we get married next Friday.'

Laura knew Sir George wouldn't allow that to happen but she didn't want to add to Caroline's fears that Richard didn't want to marry her. Instead, she said calmly, 'He won't do that, darling, and it may be a registry office wedding but you're going to make a beautiful bride.'

Laura had designed and made a white silk chiffon dress which was lined with white satin. It had a dropped waistline which was the height of fashion, with floating triangles of chiffon stitched to the skirt which showed off Caroline's perfect legs.

That night Laura hardly slept as her fears grew. Richard's cable had been upsetting. Supposing he really didn't want to marry her but was being forced by his parents to do the right thing?

The thought that her daughter was entering a marriage that was doomed from the start broke her heart. Yet she realized that the life of an unmarried mother would be hard. Where were they going to live? Was Richard's father going to bring pressure to bear and insist they live in America? Round and round her thoughts went, giving her a headache and she wished Walter was there to allay her fears. Why is he behaving so strangely? she asked herself for the hundredth time. It was obvious he'd met someone else, and her feelings of jealously increased until they consumed her.

By six o'clock in the morning she got out of bed feeling overwhelmed with worry. One thing was certain. Without waiting to be told she'd take the bull by the horns, and when he arrived in London she'd ask him outright if he wanted a divorce.

When the ship docked at Southampton Richard caught the train to London and got a taxi to take him to Green Street. Caroline wasn't meeting him at his flat in Jermyn Street until three o'clock so he had three hours to spend with his parents.

His mother would be sweet, understanding and supportive but he wasn't so sure about his father. As he neared his parents' house he realized he'd only been thinking about himself and how marriage would change his life for ever. Was Caroline harbouring the same worries and doubts? Probably not, he decided. Every girl in the world wanted to get married. That was what the season was all about. That's why debutants had coming-out balls and mothers with sons were made a fuss of by mothers with daughters. In high society he would be branded as 'not safe in taxis', but being pregnant Caroline would be called 'fast' and he hoped she wouldn't mind. Or perhaps people in her theatrical world were more broad-minded.

'So what have you got to say for yourself, you bloody fool,' grunted Sir George in a low voice so the servants wouldn't hear.

Richard had vowed to keep his dignity and act like a gentleman. 'I'm in love with Caroline, Father, and very proud of her too,' he replied. 'She comes from an aristocratic family, she's very beautiful and I'm looking forward to marrying her.'

Honor Montgomery said as she kissed him on the cheek,

'That's so lovely to hear, Richard, darling.' Her eyes brimmed with tears. 'To think that my baby boy is going to get married and you're so young, sweetheart. Never mind, we'll make the best of it and I've persuaded your father to buy you a nice house where you can set up home when you eventually return from America.'

Richard looked at his father in surprise. 'That's terribly kind of you. I'd assumed we'd live in Jermyn Street.'

'How can you live with a baby in a flat? You need staff and a nanny when you're married; otherwise life will be hell.'

Honor sat down on the sofa and patted the space beside her. 'I'm longing to meet my future daughter-in-law. Perhaps we can go house-hunting together? Her mother came to lunch; she's quite a determined person, isn't she?'

'I don't know. We only met briefly when she and her mother were staying with Lady Lizzie, as everyone calls her.' Richard's face lit up as he remembered that night when Caroline had danced for her family and he'd fallen in love with her.

'Are you truly in love with her, darling? No one will blame you if you don't want to go through with this marriage,' Honor added.

At that moment, Richard realized how much he loved and desired Caroline. He longed to share his life with her and have a family of his own. He was ready to grow up and take on the responsibility of a married man. Turning to his mother with glowing eyes, he said, 'Yes, Mama. I really love her and you must both come with me on Wednesday night to see the first night of *The Fairy Queen*. You're going to fall in love with her too when you see her dance.'

When Caroline pressed the front doorbell of Richard's flat her heart was thundering in her ears. More nervous than before a performance and more frightened than when she visited the doctor to have her pregnancy confirmed, she felt faint when she heard his footsteps coming to answer the door. Then she looked up into Richard's face.

'My darling girl,' he said, taking her in his arms and holding her tightly. She instantly burst into tears as she clung to him.

'I thought you might be angry with me,' she sobbed.

Richard picked her up in his strong arms and carried her into the bedroom of his flat as if she'd been a child.

'How could I be angry with you, sweetheart? It's my baby you're carrying and, best of all, we're getting married on Friday. You'll be my wife.'

'I know my mother went to your parents . . .' she began in apologetic tones.

Richard silenced her with a kiss. Then, looking into her eyes, he said, 'I'll admit I was a bit shocked at first but when I really thought about it I was always going to ask you to marry me because I really love you. It's just happening sooner than I'd planned. What about you and the new role you've got? Will you be able to do it now?' There was genuine concern in his voice. She looked so frail and delicate and he decided he wouldn't tell her he was bringing his parents to the first night.

Relaxed and lying on the bed beside Richard, Caroline had never felt so happy and so secure in her life. She was going to have it all. Her career, Richard to love and look after her and their baby.

'I love you so much,' she said impulsively as she wiped away the tears.

'There's only one fly in the ointment and it's a jolly big one,' he said with sudden seriousness.

'What is it?'

'While you're the toast of the town at Drury Lane I have to leave next week to sail back to New York for another three months.'

Fifteen

Diana clapped her hands in delight. It was the first time she'd seen the elegant house in London which Robert had rented for the season. 'It's beautiful, and so light and spacious,' she enthused, looking around the immaculate drawing room which overlooked the trees in the communal gardens of Royal Avenue in Chelsea. At the other end another window revealed their own private courtyard where exotic plants flourished.

'We will be able to give marvellous parties here, won't we? This is the most beautiful townhouse I've ever seen. Wait until the others see it.'

Robert smiled with relief. Diana had longed for a house in London for some time, especially when she realized what fun Laura, Lizzie and Beattie seemed to be having. There was Emily and Archie to consider, too. Her daughter was going to be presented at court in May and Archie was already at Oxford reading History, so they could invite their friends to the parties she planned to give.

'It's so beautifully furnished too,' Diana continued.

'Who are the owners? They've got such good taste,' she asked Robert as she looked around at the heavily draped brocade curtains with swagged pelmets.

'You really like it?' Robert inquired cautiously.

She looked at him curiously. 'Why do you keep asking if I like it?'

His smile broadened. 'The truth is I haven't rented it for the season.'

'Then . . .?' She stopped abruptly and looked dismayed.

He started laughing. 'I haven't rented it because I've bought it, hook, line and sinker.'

Diana gave a girlish scream of excitement as she flung her arms around him his neck. 'How? Why?' she gasped.

'I had to sell a bit of land but I knew you wanted a pied-à-terre in London. The previous owners have gone to live in Australia so I bought all the contents as well. Then I began to have nightmares in case you hated it.'

Diana looked into his eyes. 'How could I not like it, darling?' she exclaimed, kissing him. 'I'm thrilled beyond words, and Emily and Archie will adore it too. How can I ever thank you?'

Robert raised his eyebrows. 'How about another dirty weekend in Paris?' he whispered.

She laughed playfully. 'Any time, any place and anywhere, my darling!'

Later that day she decided to drop in to see Laura, who had her hands full because of Caroline's pregnancy and forthcoming marriage. When she rang the front doorbell of Laura's flat she was relieved to hear footsteps hurrying to open the door and Laura stood there, a pale shadow of her former self.

'Are you all right?' Diana asked, kissing her on the cheek. 'How is Caroline?' she added anxiously.

Laura led her into the drawing room. 'Everything is such a mess,' she said, her voice breaking. Then she told Diana about the latest developments. 'So Richard has to set sail to go back to New York the morning after the wedding. Poor Caroline is desperately upset and he'll be away for three months. Meanwhile, I have to face the prospect of Walter wanting a divorce,' she added.

'What are you talking about?' Diana asked in shocked tones. 'Your Walter? I don't believe it. He's always been devoted to you and it was you, not him, who wanted a separation.'

'Don't remind me. I think I made a big mistake. He hasn't had a drink for years and I'm sure he'll never drink again, but something is definitely going on and I think he's met another woman. When we were talking on the telephone a woman called to see him and he told the maid to show a Mrs Hamilton into the drawing room. I'm really afraid he wants to get married again.'

'That could have been a neighbour or just a friend, couldn't it?' Diana pointed out. 'When is he arriving in London?'

'Tomorrow, and you know it's Caroline first night on Wednesday.'

'My dear, we have our tickets and I can't wait to see her dance again. You know we are here for the summer?'

'Yes. You said you were going to rent a house. Is it nice?'

'It's perfect and Robert has gone and bought it as a surprise for me. We're going to be in London for as long as we like and as often as we want because of Emily and Archie.'

'That's wonderful. How lovely that we will be able to see more of you and Robert,' Laura exclaimed.

'I know, and think of the shopping sprees we can have and little luncheons at the Ritz,' Diana added gleefully.

Laura was up at dawn the next morning because she knew Walter had booked a sleeper on the overnight train from Edinburgh which would arrive at St Pancras in the early morning. She put fresh sheets on her bed, made sure the bathroom and kitchen were spotless and pumped up the cushions in the drawing room where she'd arranged a vase of roses to put on a side table.

Feeling increasingly apprehensive, she put on a becoming deep blue dress and a smart pair of shoes. When she looked at herself in the long mirror in her bedroom she realized he hadn't seen her new hairstyle. Instead of having a bun at the back and a curly fringe which was the fashion twenty years ago, she'd taken Caroline's advice and gone to a hairdresser who had cut her hair in the new short style which Beattie and Lizzie had already chosen to have. Now she wasn't sure whether Walter would approve. He used to love watching her unpinning her long hair at night.

'Your father will be here any minute,' she warned Caroline as she emerged from her room with tangled hair and a crumpled nightgown.

'So?' She shuffled to the bathroom. 'Why are you all dressed up like a dog's dinner? Dada is used to seeing us as we really are,' she protested.

Laura looked abashed. 'This is a perfectly ordinary day dress. Now, can I get you some breakfast?'

'I'll be sick if I eat anything. Why does one get sick when

you're pregnant? And why only in the morning? Today is our third full dress rehearsal so I'd better get on,' she said. 'Richard is coming to see the show today as well as on the first night, and I might stay with him at his flat. I can't bear to think he'll have gone again on Saturday.' There was a catch in her voice. 'Three months is a long time to be apart.'

'I thought you might have stayed in his flat last night.'

Caroline's eyes widened and she grinned at her mother. 'Are you encouraging me to live in sin? Oh! What would the Lord God say? Actually, Richard had to stay with his parents last night. His father said they had things to discuss. I think they're going to give him a lot of money as well as buying us a house. What with his earnings and mine, we could be very rich.'

Laura smiled fondly. 'God is very forgiving and by the sound of it your future father-in-law is very generous.'

'Oh, I do hope so,' Caroline replied, disappearing in the direction of the bathroom.

By eleven o'clock Laura was getting seriously worried that Walter hadn't arrived. Had he been taken ill? Perhaps there had been a train accident? Or maybe the taxi from the station had been involved in a crash and he'd been injured.

Caroline had left two hours ago and Laura wished one of her sisters had dropped in to see her and take her mind of her worries. Pacing around the flat, she finally decided to phone him; perhaps he was still at Dalkeith House with his lady friend.

The housekeeper answered the telephone.

'Good morning, Mrs West. Do you know which London hotel Mr Leighton-Harvey booked in to?' Laura asked.

'I'm afraid he didn't tell me, milady. He just said it was near where you live.'

'I see. Well, thank you very much.' At that moment Laura heard a taxi draw up outside and she rushed to the window. Out of the cab the tall, handsome figure of Walter emerged, still with military bearing. He looked well too as he turned and walked briskly up the front steps. For a moment Laura felt quite faint as she went to open her front door. The moment she'd been waiting for had arrived and brought with it a feeling of joy mixed with dread.

'Hello there!' he said cheerfully when he saw her waiting for him in the doorway.

'Hello, Walter.' Her heart sank. She'd never seen him looking as happy as this since . . . since they'd first fallen in love nearly twenty-five years ago. Her hunch had been right. He'd obviously met someone else. As she led the way into the drawing room his eyes sparkled and his movements were jaunty.

'I was expecting you much earlier,' Laura told him. 'I'm afraid Caroline had to leave for a dress rehearsal,' she said quietly.

'Good!' he said unexpectedly. 'You and I have things to discuss — very important things.'

Laura sat down suddenly as her legs felt they were going to give way and she felt sick.

'So . . . who is she?' Laura blurted out. 'Do I know her?'

Walter looked confused as he took a seat opposite her. 'What are you talking about?'

'I'm not a fool, Walter. You've been acting quite differently since your sister died. The other day when we were talking on the telephone some woman called to see you and you couldn't wait to see her. You barely said goodbye to me, you were in such a hurry . . .' There was a catch in her voice but she rallied, saying, 'If it's a divorce you want you can have one. This is not the first time you've caused me great pain, but I shouldn't have refused to live with you in the first place, so it's partly my fault.'

Her face crumpled and her breath caught in a sob.

Walter leaned forward in the chair and dropped to his knees before clasping her hand with a bewildered expression.

'Oh, Laura, Laura, my darling, you've got it all completely and utterly wrong. I promise you there is no woman in my life. How could there be when I've never stopped loving you? Now, will you listen to me?' he pleaded.

She nodded, unable to speak.

'When poor Rowena died I discovered she'd left everything to me including Dalkeith House and all the contents plus a lot of money. I knew she was comfortably well-off but her husband had left her a great deal more than I'd realized. The

woman who called on me when I was talking to you was Mrs
Hugh Hamilton. She has bought Dalkeith House and then she
told me last week that her husband had suggested they buy
most of the furniture. That's why I was in a hurry to see her.
Otherwise I was going to have to get an auction house to get
rid of it. Neil has gone to Australia where he's doing very well
sheep farming so I'm once again a fairly rich man and I'm
here today not just to see Caroline but more importantly to
ask you if we can become a couple again. You're the only
woman I've ever really loved and I know I let you down with
my drinking, but will you give me another chance? Please,
Laura. We can stay here or I can buy a nice house in this area,
near your sisters? What do you say, darling? Please say "yes"
and make me the happiest man on earth.'

Looking into his eyes, Laura realized there was no doubting
his honesty and sincerity. Before she had time to answer he
rose to his feet and put his hand in his coat pocket.

'The reason I'm late this morning is because once I'd dumped
my luggage in the hotel I wanted to do some shopping in
Bond Street, which took longer than I'd realized.'

He'd opened a small leather jewellery case while he was
talking, and lying on a bed of white velvet was a wide gold
wedding ring, similar to Laura's original ring. Beside it lay a
sapphire and diamond engagement ring.

'May I?' he asked, slipping off the narrow gold ring she'd
bought in a pawn shop so that no one would think she was
an unmarried mother.

'Will you share your life with me again, Laura? I can't live
any longer without you.'

Overcome with emotion, she got to her feet and flung her
arms around him as she pressed her wet cheek against his face.
Holding her tightly, she heard him say, 'The woman in my
life is and always will be you, Laura, darling. Now that we're
together again I'm never going to let you go.'

Then he kissed her with passion and a wave of desire swept
through her, something that hadn't happened since she'd been
a young woman.

'Why don't you cancel that hotel and stay with me?' she
whispered. 'Caroline will be staying with Richard tonight.'

He gazed into her eyes. 'That, my darling Laura, is the most intelligent thing I think you've ever said.'

'Look at these reviews,' Walter exclaimed triumphantly. He'd gone to a local shop as soon as it opened and bought a copy of every newspaper in order to see what the critics had written about the first night of *The Fairy Queen*.

'Do read them aloud to me,' Laura replied excitedly as she made their breakfast.

Walter cleared his throat. '"The prima ballerina, Caroline Harvey moves with exquisite precision and grace and shows promise of a great future."' He put down the newspaper and picked up another one. '"The young solo dancer, Caroline Harvey, gives a breath-taking performance as the Fairy Queen . . ." Now listen to this one in the *Telegraph*,' he said with pride. '"Caroline Harvey's performance was magical, a blend of poetic grace and beauty. New on the scene, she could become another Anna Pavlova."'

He looked up at Laura as she toasted the bread.

'You've made her what she is today and I'm so sorry I was such a rotten father. If I could have the last few years over again I would have handled everything differently instead of leaving it all to you.'

Laura reached out and took his hand. 'You were there for her, Walter. She loved going to stay with you and it's wonderful for both she and me that you're well and with us now. I'll never forget her excitement when we told her we were together again. It's the best thing that's happened to both her and me.'

Walter held her hand and looking down at the rings he'd given her the previous day he spoke with sincerity.

'I have to do a lot to make up for the lost years we could have shared together. I never stopped loving you and I want to buy you a house and look after you which I should have done all along. Will you ever really forgive my madness and my badness?'

She smiled and looked into his eyes. 'I think I forgave you a very long time ago although I didn't realize it. You were in the clutches of a demon and didn't realize you were killing yourself.'

'It's all in the past now so let's live for today and the future.'

At the Drury Lane Theatre the previous evening her sisters had been staggered to see her looking twenty years younger, hanging on to Walter's arm as she beamed with happiness. Beattie had been the first to notice the sapphire and diamond ring next to the wide gold wedding ring.

'Where did they come from?' Lizzie had asked accusingly.

Diana had exclaimed, 'They really suit you, Laura.'

It was with serene pleasure that Laura was able to say, 'Walter and I are together again and he gave them to me.'

Caroline lay exhausted in Richard's bed as he read aloud the reviews of *The Fairy Queen*. All her dreams had come true and yet she had a feeling of anti-climax. For years she'd studied ballet dancing and now that she'd succeeded she began to wonder if it had all been worthwhile? Having this baby was going to ruin her figure and age her in general and she suddenly felt angry with Richard for letting it happen. She'd no longer be the slim and lissom ingénue who had stormed to the top of her profession.

Feelings of discontent still swept through her, as they'd done all her life, and she refused to believe what her father had said when she was fifteen that her expectations were pitched too high.

'If you aim for the stars you may hit the barn roof,' Walter had told her, 'and be grateful you got that far.'

Nothing was ever enough to satisfy Caroline. Tomorrow morning she'd become Mrs Richard Montgomery, and her future husband was handsome, loving and his parents wealthy enough to buy them a house in Mayfair, so what more did she want in life? Not a baby, for a start, and she felt blighted by her pregnancy. The truth was that nothing in her life had lived up to her expectations and now she felt that nothing ever would.

'What marvellous reviews,' Richard said warmly. 'I'm so proud of you, darling.'

Caroline sat up in the bed and punched a pillow angrily. 'It's easy for you to sit there and read the newspapers. I've got to perform every bloody night no matter how sick or tired I am and it's all your fault.'

'I don't think you can blame me for everything,' he retorted. 'I've had to adjust to our present circumstances too, you know.'

'So you think I got pregnant in order to make a good marriage, do you?' she snapped pettishly. 'All I wanted was a career in ballet and now I'm landed with a baby and marriage.'

Her face was pink with anger and Richard saw a side of her that shocked him.

'Am I to understand that you'd rather not marry me?' he asked coldly.

'Do what you bloody well like. As it is, you're going back to New York as soon as we're married where you will no doubt chase after every girl you meet!' As she gave vent to her anger she was struggling into her clothes and gathering up her make-up before stuffing it into her large handbag.

'What are you doing?' he asked angrily.

'Getting out of here. Your parents look down on me because I'm on the stage so they'll be delighted if I call off the marriage . . .' Tears were flowing down her face now and, wrenching open the door of his flat, she fled the scene, leaving Richard aghast. They were supposed to be getting married the next morning and he shuddered at the thought of the ensuing chaos if she didn't turn up at Caxton Hall.

Laura and Walter had finished breakfast and were settling down to read the newspapers when Caroline came hurtling into the flat, her face blotched with crying.

'What's the matter?' Laura asked in dismay.

'Everything is such a mess,' Caroline sobbed. 'I think I've cancelled the wedding tomorrow.'

Walter winked at Laura before saying, 'Is that all? I thought for a moment you had a serious problem. So you really don't want to marry that nice young man who loves you? Is that it, my darling girl?'

Laura watched as Walter led Caroline to the sofa where he sat down beside her, talking to her quietly and calmly.

'You've got a lot on your plate what with the stress of being the solo ballerina every night as well as expecting a baby and getting married tomorrow.' He stroked her hair as he'd done when she'd been a child.

'Does Richard really want to marry me, though?' she asked.

Walter smiled. 'Well, I don't think he hurriedly crossed the Atlantic to buy himself a new suit. Of course he loves you, and you love him too. Isn't that right?'

While Laura went to the kitchen to make cups of tea for them all she marvelled at the way Caroline's father handled her and soothed her so that after a while she was smiling again as she leaned against Walter with her head resting on his shoulder.

Their close relationship made Laura realize – and not for the first time – that maybe she'd been too lenient with her daughter, partly for the sake of peace, but also because she'd been deprived of everything her rich cousins had taken for granted.

Walter joined Laura in the kitchen while Caroline went to have a bath. Sliding his arm around her waist, he whispered, 'It's all quiet on the Western Front. She's telephoning Richard to apologize and assure him that she'll be at Caxton Hall.'

'Thank God.' Laura breathed a sigh of relief.

'Too much has been happening in her life so I'm not surprised she became overwrought. It's probably a good thing that he's returning to America. By the time he gets back she'll have stopped performing and her life won't be so hectic.'

Laura gave him a knowing look. 'I hope you're right,' she whispered back.

In a show of family loyalty all the Fairbairn sisters arrived in good time at Caxton Hall accompanied by their husbands and children. It was, after all, the marriage of the late Earl and Countess of Rothbury's first grandchild, so no one mentioned the expected baby. Laura had been desperately keen to make the whole day a joyous affair so after the marriage she'd arranged a buffet lunch in Beattie's house and Walter had secured tickets for *The Fairy Queen*, which added to the excitement.

Georgie and Shane had been the first to arrive with their family, which now numbered two daughters and four sons.

Then Diana and Robert arrived with Emily and Archie, joined minutes later by Lizzie and Humphrey accompanied by Isabel, Rose and Emma. Margaret, it was explained, was ill in bed with influenza, which nobody believed. Flora, Alice and her husband Colin had travelled down from Scotland, to be warmly greeted by Beattie and Andrew, who were accompanied by Henry, Kathleen and Camilla.

'We didn't bring Philip,' Beattie explained. 'We were afraid he'd start yelling.'

'And he's got a strong pair of lungs,' Andrew added proudly.

When Richard stepped out of a Daimler followed by Sir George and Lady Montgomery there was an outbreak of nudging and whispering among the Fairbairns. The Montgomeries had only invited a dozen friends, and both George and Honor looked appalled at the packed registry office.

'What an enormous family,' Honor whispered in dismay. Georgie heard the remark and, leaning forward, she spoke in a loud voice.

'This beats a funeral, doesn't it? We've had a couple of those and it's nice to have a big family around you.' Then she turned to Lizzie and said in clear tones. 'Who is that stuck-up cow?'

At that moment Caroline arrived, followed by Laura and Walter. Wearing the white chiffon dress her mother had made and with small white flowers woven into her hair, she drew gasps of admiration, especially from her young cousins. They had never seen such beauty in the family, and for Caroline it was the most satisfying moment in her life. She'd always been jealous of her cousins but now she had no need. She'd become a prima ballerina and she was making a good marriage; there was no reason to envy them any more.

Walking over to Richard's side, she smiled up at him and he smiled back as he slipped his arm around her waist. Then the registrar asked them to be seated and the formal procedure of a civil marriage took place. Laura watched Caroline and wished they were all in church, with a clergyman to guide them through their vows before God.

When the couple emerged first from Caxton Hall they were met with a barrage of flashlight cameras and yells of 'look this way' and 'how about kissing your bride?'

Richard kissed his new wife with ardour and they started laughing with sheer happiness.

Several of the other dancers had come to watch the star of the show get spliced and now murmured: 'The show will run for months now after all this publicity.'

Honor Montgomery turned to her husband as they waited for their car and remarked, 'It's all been terribly theatrical, hasn't it? She's really just a showgirl.'

Sir George was flushed and exuded enthusiasm. 'But what a showgirl! No wonder Richard fell hook, line and sinker for her! Just look at those legs!'

Honor turned sharply away, her mouth drawn into a tight line of disapproval. In that moment she decided she hated her new daughter-in-law.

The staff at Beattie's house were standing ready for the arrival of the family for the buffet luncheon. The champagne was on ice, the chef was putting the finishing touches to the caviar canapés, the fresh salmon was arranged on great platters and there was a variety of salads. Laura had even ordered a two-tier wedding cake and there was an abundance of strawberries and ice cream for the younger cousins.

As she and Walter arrived at the Belgrave Square house she said to him, 'I'm just going to have a word with the chef to make sure everything is under control.'

Walter smiled at her and gave her a kiss on the cheek. 'Relax, my darling. You need a break. What about a weekend in Venice before we start house hunting?'

Laura was about to refuse because she couldn't leave Caroline alone for a few days, but then she thought, why not? Her daughter was now a married woman and she could always stay with Diana. She turned to Walter, her eyes sparkling. 'That's a brilliant idea. I've always longed to go to Venice.'

One of the waiters was topping up champagne glasses and directing guests to the dining room where luncheon was being served when Colin came up to Laura and asked if he could have a word with her in private. Laura looked up at him in surprise. Alice's husband was a quiet and shy clergyman and she'd never had the opportunity to get to know him.

'Shall we go outside on to the balcony?' Colin suggested as Walter joined them. 'I was wondering if you'd like me to arrange a service for blessing the marriage of Caroline and Richard up at Lochlee, after Caroline has given birth to their baby?'

Laura's face lit up and she looked at Walter. 'What a wonderful idea.'

'It's a brilliant idea,' he agreed. 'We could have hymns and it would be a real church wedding.'

Colin's eyes shone with delight. 'You do realize I can't conduct the actual marriage ceremony but I can give a blessing, which Caroline deserves and it will be very meaningful.'

Laura beamed. Caroline was going to have the white wedding she'd really wanted after all. 'That is wonderful, and thank you so much for suggesting it, Colin. Do go and tell Caroline. I know she will be thrilled.'

Colin hesitated, then said, 'I hope you don't think I'm being pushy, but I could also christen their baby after the blessing.'

Walter patted him on the back and spoke earnestly. 'I think you're one of the nicest brothers-in-law Laura has. I've been lucky enough to be accepted into the Fairbairn family again after a long absence and I'm looking forward to getting to know you better. Laura and I are also very grateful that you haven't condemned Caroline for getting pregnant out of wedlock.'

Colin blushed at the compliments. 'It's not up to me to make judgements,' he replied gently before slipping quietly into the crowded drawing room.

Looking around as she stood beside Walter, Laura watched her large family with pride. The merry clink of champagne glasses, the laughter and the gaiety of the conversation was heart-warming.

The sisters had come a long way from their origins in the grandeur of Lochlee Castle, and apart from losing the son and heir in squalid circumstances, and the second son in the Boer War, the girls remained devoted to each other and had made successes of their lives. They'd managed to survive many a storm too. Eleanor had died in a terrible accident, while Catriona had suffered a breakdown when their mother died and had committed suicide.

The other seven had survived the Great War in 1914 though,

along with ruinous death duties, bankruptcy, love affairs and
near death in childbirth. The future would gradually be taken
over by all their many children, and within months Laura
would be the first to become a grandmother.

A new era was dawning.